a life lived
beautifully

BOOKS BY CATHERINE MILLER

a life lived beautifully

CATHERINE MILLER

Bookouture

Published by Bookouture in 2023

An imprint of Storyfire Ltd.
Carmelite House
50 Victoria Embankment
London EC4Y 0DZ

www.bookouture.com

ISBN: 978-1-83790-908-7
eBook ISBN: 978-1-80314-765-9

As I don't have any sisters, I'm dedicating this to some of the women who've always been like sisters to me: The Romaniacs and Sarah Carnell

PROLOGUE

There are some things that once divided can never be put back together. Like a walnut shell, that once crushed in two can never be whole again. The fractures still evident even with the use of superglue. The world has a tendency to shift like that, when we least expect it. In some cases it can be the worst thing in the world, but in others, it's the start of something wonderful. We all hope our divides will be the wonderful kind.

For Jodie and Harper Quinlan, without the divide they wouldn't both exist. Twenty-three chromosomes that duplicated into a perfect copy. Two embryos that were originally destined to be one. And as two halves of a whole they went on and shared an amniotic sac, as well as everything else going forward. Their birthday. Their christening day. Their first day at school.

Because even though they had divided, Jodie and Harper were inseparable. They'd heard the phrase 'two peas in a pod' so often that their mother, Francesca, had T-shirts made when they were toddlers. With their long, straight, white-blonde hair and their striking blue eyes they were so often mistaken for each other (by their friends, their teachers, the local shopkeeper, even their own grandparents – the list was endless) that they were in the habit of wearing different coloured hairbands. Jodie wore yellow and Harper wore red. Or one had their hair up and the other down, with their partings in different directions.

These were habits that had started when they'd joined preschool, their mother wanting to make a distinction between them, and had continued when they'd started doing their own hair. It had lasted through secondary school and into university, where they were both studying dance. Because, of course, they left home together to go and study the same subject.

They'd tried not having their hair system in place on occasion. But within no time at all they were both fed up with correcting people on who was who, including, at times, their parents.

They often had conversations about when they'd no longer need their hair accessories to differentiate them. About when they might live in different places and have different groups of friends. But that wasn't something they truly desired. What they both loved to do was dance and perform, and they'd promised each other a lifetime of dancing together.

And now, after years of training, they were on the cusp of that dream becoming a reality. Fresh-faced and twenty-one, they were heading to London to star in their first production. It wasn't quite the ultimate dream – that would be headlining a West End show – but every role they landed would be a step in the right direction. This time it was starring in the chorus, on the outskirts of the West End. A start that so many performers wished for. And they knew, in part, that being identical twins with Scandi-blonde hair and blue eyes had swung the audition for them. 'Two for the price of one,' the casting director had joked to his colleagues, although fortunately two contracts had been forthcoming, despite the jest. They were on their way. They were about to fulfil the dream they'd spent years working towards. They were about to enter a highlight of their lives.

What they didn't know was that there was another divide waiting for them. One that would provide a far bigger seismic shift. One that would make wearing the correct hairband seem insignificant. Because while some divides are wonderful, others define the paths of our lives. Jodie and Harper. Harper and Jodie. Peas in a pod. About to start a new life together in London.

Until...

CHAPTER ONE

JODIE

With a week of performances under her belt, Jodie still hadn't got used to the explosion of applause at the end of each show. Each time it had taken her by surprise, and tonight was no different. She waited on her spot on the stage, her sister by her side, until it was their turn, along with the rest of the chorus, to step forwards and take their bow.

Every single member of the audience was on their feet whooping and cheering, and the noise and the lights took her breath away. When she was on stage she liked to pretend there was no one watching, so it was always a surprise to be faced with a full auditorium.

The production was a modern-day interpretation of Hansel and Gretel turned into a musical with the shortened and somewhat abstract title *Gingerbread*. The initial audience figures and feedback were beyond anything their director, Guy May, had hoped for. After every performance this week he'd been ecstatic, as if what had occurred on stage had actually injected fuel into his blood.

Jodie could understand why. Even standing on this stage, playing a small part in this big production, felt significant. As if they were all part of a show that was going to get bigger and better. It was a month-long run at the Witlow Theatre on the outskirts of Stratford in the East End of London. It didn't class as a West End theatre, but it was one of the theatres used as a tester venue. The investors needed to know how a show would perform and the whole cast were aware that this was a litmus test. It would give an indicator of how well the show could do over a longer period if it were to tour to one of the bigger theatres. It wasn't just the audience paying attention to how well *Gingerbread* was going. So far, the early reviews had been outstanding, and the shows had been packed.

Jodie took her bow. Her sister, her five-foot-eight carbon copy, folded her body beside her. Even the way they did that was identical. People often commented on their synchronicity. It was only their personalities that told them apart. Harper, the more organised of the two, always arranging checklists and making sure they were prepared, with Jodie always more laid-back. If one of them had a map in hand, it was a clear indictor that it was Harper. But right now, their deep breaths matched each other as they recovered from the final dance.

The curtain came down in front of the whole crew, with various members adding their own whoops to the cheers coming from the audience, excitement pulsing in the air.

'Again!' Guy said, indicating that the whole cast should take another bow.

It wasn't something they did every night, but he clearly wanted to celebrate the end of a successful week. Tomorrow was Monday and would be their first day off. Their only full scheduled day off each week.

Obligingly, the curtain rose and the audience who'd been yelling '*Encore!*' gave a delighted standing ovation as the whole cast and crew took their bows again at the centre of the stage.

Jodie loved the rush of a live performance. Even though she liked to pretend no one was there, that was just a trick to steady her nerves. In truth, it wouldn't be the same without people there to watch. The streak of tension it created pushed her to do her best. And experiencing the audience's appreciation, not through that inevitable, steady, polite applause, but in the toe-tapping, arm-waving, rapturous on-their-feet type of applause, was blowing her mind in the best possible way. Especially as this wasn't a one-off. It had happened at the end of every performance this week and the buzz of being part of it was immense.

Jodie glanced at Harper, her counterpart, knowing she felt the same glow inside. They took the few steps towards the front of the stage and took their second bow of the night.

After each performance this week, they'd not been able to sleep once they'd returned to their rented flat. The adrenalin high had been coursing through their systems too intensely to just switch off as soon as they got back. Instead, they'd gathered on the sofa to analyse how everything had gone, with Harper taking notes. Whether they'd timed their moves to perfection, whether they'd managed to hit each note, whether there was anything they'd want to do differently for the next show. They weren't really in need of any director's notes when they'd become so good at providing their own post-show analysis. On these evenings, Jodie imagined her sister as a director in the future. Harper was methodical enough, that was for certain, whereas Jodie just joined in as a way of unwinding.

The tremendous sound of the applause made Jodie focus on the moment. It continued as they straightened up, the last of the cast to do so. The stage hands soon followed and then it was time for the curtain to descend for a final time that week. Jodie could get used to this. She already felt like she *was* getting used to this, confident in the knowledge that she and Harper were destined for bigger and better things. They wouldn't always be the last names in the programme. The time would come when they would be the headliners.

'Amazing!' Guy said as he turned to face everyone. 'We

need to celebrate. Everyone get changed and we'll meet in the lobby once it's cleared.'

Jodie and Harper followed everyone else to the changing rooms, the excitement palpable. They got themselves sorted and downed a bottle of water each, before continuing like sheep into the foyer. There were a few audience members hanging around hoping to see the cast, and the stars Ryland and Patsy signed their programmes with delight while every remaining cast member watched on, dreaming of the time when that would be them.

'We need a celebratory drink after such a successful first week,' said Guy. 'Let's head to the pub over the road. And I want everyone to help me start a new tradition. I want you all to take turns dancing your way across the road.'

The ushers looked hopeful that they might get an invite, but Guy was far too obnoxious to notice such things and instead strode out as if he were leading an expedition.

The cast snaked in a line behind him, obliging him because, really, they had no choice. But they all knew that after the tense months of rehearsals and the pressure to get it right, this truly was an achievement to celebrate. The first week had been a resounding success and nothing more could be asked of them until next week.

The East London side street was nearly deserted now the audience had dissipated, and as it led nowhere, it was almost devoid of traffic. Patsy danced across the road, as requested by Guy, performing a series of pirouettes until she reached the other kerb. It reminded Jodie of the ballerina figure she'd had in her old jewellery box as a child, each move carried out to perfection. Everyone had stopped to watch, despite the drizzle, then burst into a round of spontaneous applause at her mini performance.

Of course, Ryland being the other lead, he followed next

with a leap and a mini break dance that got him to the other side.

Once Ryland and Patsy were reunited, they each spread an arm out, inviting everyone else to take part. The stage was no longer in the theatre. It was the road they had to cross, and now it had to be done with a flourish. Especially with their director watching from the entrance to the pub. It was a chance to impress.

The order in which they danced across almost exactly reflected the order of their names in the programme. A hierarchy that had occurred in the theatre and wasn't falling away now they were outside. Although with Jodie before Harper, it wasn't quite alphabetically correct. They just had to hope their different coloured jogging bottoms provided enough of a distinction between them to help the cast out.

Jodie was left with the same dilemma as everyone else: how to go about crossing the road? How to make themselves stand out so that the next time their director had to select someone to be an understudy or to cover the lead, they'd be at the forefront of his mind?

In her head, Jodie settled for the butterfly, an extremely difficult ballet move that not every dancer was capable of. She'd not had the chance to demonstrate the fullness of her abilities and this felt like the moment to do just that.

If the adrenalin wasn't already there from the evening's performance, then this would certainly have cranked it up to a peak. She glanced at Harper, wishing their twin connection really did include the ability to read each other's thoughts. On occasion, they'd do similar things, like eat the same lunch when not together, but despite trying, they'd never perfected staring into each other's eyes and reading one another's mind. It was a pity, because in this moment, Jodie would really love to know what Harper was planning to do.

The tension on this side of the pavement was evident and

there was no conferring going on. Everyone wanted to outdo one another. In that moment, Jodie couldn't work out if she also wanted to outdo Harper.

They observed various efforts. Some copying what had gone before. Others trying to do amazing things only to fail. Jodie was beginning to grade the various moves, trying not to talk herself out of what she planned to try. Before she could, she was on the edge of the pavement, everyone waiting for her to take her turn.

She launched into the move, spinning once then again before lifting off the floor, her chest forwards and all her limbs bent behind her to form the shape of a butterfly, completing a turn in the air as if she were capable of flight. It lasted milliseconds, but it felt longer as she unfurled, landing perfectly on the ground, crouching with her knee bent as if she were worshipping at Guy's feet, who'd ventured away from the pub door to the kerb.

The cast burst into applause, as did a few passers-by who'd stopped to watch this strange spectacle. Jodie basked in the applause for a moment before remembering this wasn't a stage. It was a London street, and her sister was up next. She scrabbled to the pavement in an effort not to miss her sister's turn.

It shouldn't have been a surprise that she was attempting the same move. Maybe their twinstincts were strong enough to read each other's minds after all. If they'd decided on the same thing, then Harper wouldn't have had much time to change her mind, and there was no time to hesitate.

Harper took flight, and if Jodie didn't know any better, she could have been watching a recording of herself, the only difference being Harper's black joggers instead of the grey she was wearing. The big propulsion into launch. The push back of all four limbs while opening up the chest. The complete rotation in the air before preparing to land.

It was as Harper stretched her right foot out ready to land, another imminent impact became apparent.

Jodie had been so focussed on her sister that she'd not spotted the black cab that had launched itself around the corner at speed. So fast that the butterfly in flight had no chance to change direction...

And before either of Harper's feet touched the ground, she was punched out of the sky. Her form changed from dancing butterfly to human trapped under a taxi too quickly for anyone to react. There was a beat. Maybe as many as three in which no one responded. There was no noise. No one moved. No shouting or screaming. No hurried phone calls. Only disbelief at what they'd just witnessed.

Staring at the crumpled form of her mirror image, Jodie, like everyone else, took more than a beat to catch up. She wasn't watching a video of herself on her phone. This was real life. Her sister was broken on the floor and she needed to respond.

And as if someone had switched off the delay, everyone reacted at once, surging forwards to pick up the broken butterfly.

Only there would be no picking her up. There would be no putting her back together. There would be none of the things they'd expected from this point onwards. Instead, there would be emergency sirens. There would be X-rays and scans and more medics than most people meet in a lifetime.

Because, when they hadn't seen it coming, the divide had happened. The thing that would separate them turned out to be a black cab on a London side street. Jodie and Harper. Harper and Jodie. Two peas in a pod.

Jodie.

Harper.

The inseparable separated.

CHAPTER TWO

HARPER

There had been many things on Harper's mind when she'd launched herself into the air. Her position. The risk of mucking up the dance move her twin sister had just performed perfectly. What she'd have to drink when they got to the bar. A black cab appearing on the seemingly empty side road hadn't been one of them. With over twenty people having performed various spins and twists and leaps without a vehicle passing them, she'd really not had any expectation of one shunting her out of the air.

But it had. And since that moment she'd met more health-care professionals and had more tests than she'd ever had in her life. Previously, the worst injury she'd sustained was a green-stick fracture after overbalancing on her roller skates when she'd been ten.

This was much worse. Of course it was. Because it was three weeks later and, while the significant purple bruising on her back and legs was beginning to fade to a plethora of assorted colours – greens and yellows and blues like she'd never seen – the feeling in her legs hadn't returned. And while there had been murmurs about the possibility of things improving once the swelling went down, as her rainbow bruises progressed, she knew not to hold on to any hope. Because somehow she knew the damage was permanent. That the hours of surgery they'd performed to try and fix her broken spine hadn't been enough.

For now, Harper was choosing to be grateful for small mercies. The fact that her butterfly jump had been high enough to result in her being a T12 paraplegic being one of them. She was doing her best not to dwell on the fact she'd never be able to jump like that again. She'd not mourned this yet; it was hard to process what was happening to her while being on a ward that was constantly busy. She wouldn't be here for much longer, though. They were all set to get her to a rehabilitation unit, but trying to communicate that to her sister was proving difficult. She seemed a million miles away.

'Did you hear what I said?' Harper tried to clarify, given that Jodie hadn't responded.

There had been a lot of that over the last couple of weeks. Jodie staring blankly ahead and not taking things in. It was as if she'd been the one to have had a knock to the head. Harper was beginning to wonder how long the shock would last because, surely, much like her bruising, it should be starting to subside by now.

In truth, Harper knew Jodie was exhausted. She hadn't been given a break from the show and she was visiting Harper daily to make up for their flaky parents, who, having taken up a campervan life, were visiting for a couple of days at a time before taking themselves off for another mini trip, despite one of their daughters being in hospital.

'No, sorry. Can you tell me again?'

'Are you okay? You seem distracted?'

'I'm sorry.' Jodie pushed herself forwards and rubbed her face as if she'd just woken up. 'I'm just wiped out. With everything that's happened and continuing with the show, I feel like I've become the definition of burning the candle at both ends.

But don't worry about me. I'll sleep on the bus on the way to the theatre.'

'Are you getting *any* sleep?' Harper recalled how late they'd been going to bed that first week, unable to wind down immediately after the performance. She'd been the one to insist that her sister continue with the show when their director had more or less demanded that she return. Harper hadn't wanted Jodie's dreams to be wiped out at the same time as hers.

'Yes, some. But don't be worrying about me. Tell me again what you were saying about rehab.'

Harper took in the vision of her twin. They weren't so identical any more. Not when she'd never be able to join in as their mum marked their heights on their old bedroom wall. Although that wasn't something they'd do now in adulthood, and if either of them were pining to go back to their childhood home, they wouldn't be able to. Not when their parents had sold up and purchased a campervan as soon as they'd left home to study dance at university. Their parents had returned from Europe as soon as they'd heard about Harper's accident, but with the cost of parking so high in London (and their tendency to complain about spending money at every juncture), they were letting Jodie play parent during much of the week. Not much change there. The twins had been the ones looking out for each other since they'd started becoming independent in their teen years. They loved their parents dearly, but they weren't the people they'd call in an emergency. They'd always had each other down as their next-of-kin.

Because of their new differences, none of the nurses ever had any difficulty working out who was who. Harper hadn't worried about helping others distinguish between them since this had happened. The dark circles under Jodie's eyes gave a distinction that had never previously been there. And there was the fact that Harper no longer had the use of her lower limbs.

'They want to send me to a specialist spinal rehabilitation

unit. It'll be for six solid weeks of intensive training to get me more independent with wheelchair use and everything else that I need to learn.'

'Really? But I thought they were still hoping...'

'Look, as a miracle hasn't presented itself thus far, I'm not expecting it to now. They wouldn't be talking about transferring me to this place if they had any expectation of me getting up and walking out of here. There will be some partial if not complete damage that I'm going to have to learn to live with.'

To everyone's shock, Harper was being very practical over her injury. She didn't see the point of not being. It wasn't like she could erase what had happened. Given the exact same scenario, she would do the same again. She would still leap and be a butterfly. She didn't even wish her sister had let her go first. This was her destiny. No one else's.

'When?'

'Not yet, but soon. It isn't in London. It's further out. That made me think... and don't take this the wrong way, but it might give you the chance to have a break from me. From visiting me, that is. It's further away so you won't be able to pop by daily like you do now, and I'm going to need to focus on my rehabilitation. It might do us good to have some time apart.'

Harper focussed on her sister's response, but she was staring blankly at her again.

'How long will it be for?'

'Six weeks of intensive rehab, like I said.'

'And you don't want to see me for the whole six weeks?'

'It's not that I don't *want* to see you. You're my twin sister, so of course I do, but for the first time in our lives we're going through different things. This isn't something where you can come along for the ride. I need to do this and you need to concentrate on living out the dream we've always shared. At least one of us gets to do that.' Harper knew her life had changed completely. She needed to adjust. They both did.

'Can I come and see you on my day off?'

'It's too far away for a quick day trip. It's a specialist unit. I think, for a short period of time, you need to reserve your energy just for you. The same as I do.'

Harper didn't want to tell her how hard it was to see her at the moment. Even Jodie's ability to walk in and walk out grated on her new state of being. She didn't want it to be that way, but it was like watching the story of how things could be, but knowing she'd never be able to walk out of a room again in the same way her identical sister could. And she didn't want to be faced with having to mourn that freedom. She wanted to get to understand her new body. She wanted to know what it was capable of without a very direct reminder of what it had once been able to do.

'But you're not leaving to go there yet?'

'No, and when I find out, I'll let you know. I won't be going without saying goodbye.'

'Okay.'

'Okay, so you're happy for us to have a break?' Harper wanted to clarify this.

'I wouldn't say I'm *happy*, but if there's no other way, then so be it.' Jodie sounded like a wounded child. One who hadn't got their way. But that was no surprise, not when neither of them had got their way. This wasn't something either of them ever expected.

But Harper couldn't concentrate on the fractures that didn't belong to her. She didn't want to think about the life that could have been. That would be too heartbreaking by far. So instead, she was going to concentrate on the things she could do.

She'd get stronger, and to start with she'd focus on learning to sit upright without assistance. It was up to her sister to live their dream right now, and even though she wasn't going to say it out loud, she hoped her sister knew that, for now at least, she couldn't watch on and be happy.

Happiness seemed a long way off. For both of them.

CHAPTER THREE

JODIE

The past few weeks had been the worst of Jodie's life. But every time she thought that, she reminded herself it was nothing compared to what had happened to Harper.

It wasn't. But that didn't take away from the fact that her life had been torn apart too. Harper was the stable base that she depended on, the one their parents had never provided. Even with what had happened, they hadn't given up campervan life, going off for days and weeks at a time. So Jodie was as alone as she'd ever been. Not least because their parents' rare visits were only extending to Harper.

Tonight was the last night of the show. After the successful first week, it was as if it had been hit by a curse. The fallout of Harper's accident had echoed among the cast. Unspoken for the most part, but loud all the same.

The accident had made the news, and the good reviews had been replaced by the tale of the tragic accident that had felled one of the cast. Rather than the five-star appraisals Guy had been expecting, he'd been faced with articles about road safety around theatres and how stage doors sometimes opened straight onto the street. And because he'd encouraged the cast to dance across the road, fingers were pointing in his direction.

'Whoever wrote that doesn't even know what door we came out of!' he'd screamed at the entire cast the day that article had come out, mumbling about shoddy journalism for several hours after.

For Jodie, there had been a strange disconnect. She was so used to having Harper within her reach that she felt as if she'd turned up at the wrong airport and missed her flight. It was disorientating in a way she couldn't fathom because it had never happened before. Harper had never not been there. What made it worse was that she was expected to carry on as usual. The show must go on, but her show was partly axed. Harper wasn't there to perform on the stage with her as usual, and it had now been confirmed that the damage was permanent. For the first time in her life, Jodie was having to go solo. It wasn't a welcome feeling.

Not that Guy seemed to care. With every day that passed it became clearer to Jodie that the cast were his minions. They were there to do his bidding to satisfy what he wanted from the show and nothing more. He'd not even signed the card they'd got for Harper. Outside this production, it was unlikely he'd even remember their names, only the parts they'd played. Or perhaps he would remember Jodie because, rather than being sympathetic towards her, it often felt like he blamed *her* for Harper's accident. That was never openly said, of course, but she sensed it in every interaction she had with him. Every time all the seats weren't full. Every time the audience's response wasn't as rapturous as that first week. Every time he looked at Jodie, he was reminded of the consequences of Harper's accident and why his show was in the papers for the wrong reasons.

'Tonight, I need you to give it your *all*,' Guy said to the cast. He didn't give pre-show pep talks every night, only when there was someone important in the audience. It was a pattern the entire cast had caught on to. 'We want to go out with a bang. We want to secure funding for another run.'

They'd heard this several times before. Only every time it was repeated, it was like it lost power. The hope gradually disintegrating before them. Jodie wouldn't have been surprised if Guy crumbled at the same time. She couldn't help but feel it was a touch of karma for not seeming to care too much about the ruined career of a twenty-one-year-old more than his precious show.

On stage, Jodie sang the required lyrics and danced the required moves, but there was no passion in what she was doing. Her passion had been squashed on that roadside. Or perhaps it had vacated when Guy had pointed out she had a contract to fulfil, even though her sister was paralysed in a hospital bed. What kind of heartless moron expected a person to return after one scheduled day off when their twin sister – her DNA counterpart – had just been so severely injured she was unable to feel her lower limbs? Guy May was who. So ever since then she'd vowed to do her job and nothing more. Once the contract was finished, she didn't plan to stay on, even if the show did end up with that elusive funding.

The same feeling seemed to have settled across all the cast. If one member of the crew had suffered something so life-changing and their director hadn't even rallied everyone to sign a sympathy card (it had been the other way round, instead), it indicated how little he cared about them. And in turn, they'd lost their passion for the show. As they took their final bow, there was no call from their director to go again.

Instead, there was a strange dullness as the curtain descended for the final time. They were all frozen in their positions as if they were street artists waiting for a coin to drop in their bowl before they'd be able to move again. Slowly, they uncreased. A step, then two, away from the stage.

'Are you going to be okay?' Dakshina asked. She was one of the other chorus girls, and the most supportive of the lot.

Jodie shrugged. 'I'm not sure.'

In the month since Harper's accident, none of them had suggested an after-show drink. They'd not even arranged it for tonight. Even though it was a normal part of a show run, it was never going to be part of this one again. Not one of them had visited her at the hospital, but Jodie was glad her sister had been afforded this respect.

'Do you want to come back to mine?' Dakshina knew Jodie would be returning to an empty flat otherwise.

Jodie had spent time at Dakshina's house before, and she decided to take up the offer again to quell the loneliness tonight.

'Sure. For a bit.'

Dakshina lived with her family. Three sisters and a brother, her parents and their widowed grandfather. They were constantly ribbing her about being a dancer in that strange way that families sometimes did. Jodie could tell it was their way of saying they were immensely proud of her, but without admitting as much. It had been a welcome distraction in the last couple of weeks to be among Dakshina's family, and she knew after tonight it might never happen again.

'What are you going to do now the run is over?' Dakshina asked after sneaking two plates of food up to the bedroom she shared with her sisters.

Jodie already knew from previous visits that Dakshina would be in trouble with her mother for eating upstairs, but Dakshina had argued that she and Jodie needed to refuel after their performance. If they did so quietly and tidily, they should get away with it.

'I don't know. Harper is being sent off for six weeks of rehab. She wants me to carry on trying to live the dream.'

'What do you want to do?'

Jodie scooped up the rice and lentil curry with her fingers, making sure not to gather too much. It was her friend's traditional way of eating, and now, on her third attempt, she was beginning to get the hang of it. 'I honestly don't know.'

'You must have some idea? Have you told Harper about the show ending?'

Jodie chewed her food, not able to answer immediately and, in that pause, Dakshina worked it out.

'You haven't told her, have you?'

Jodie shook her head. 'She has enough on her plate without worrying about the fact I'm unemployed already. At the time of her accident the show was going brilliantly. She doesn't need to know that it was downhill from that point onwards. I'll work something out.'

'There's an open audition for a pantomime tomorrow if you want to come and join me for that?'

'A *pantomime!*' Jodie had meant to say it in her head only, but the exclamation was loud and clear.

'Yes. It's another solid couple of months of work, if either of us get it.'

It wasn't exactly the dream. Nor was it the next step she'd been hoping to take because she'd never envisaged a goal that didn't include Harper by her side.

'Beggars can't be choosers, huh?'

'Dreams have got to start somewhere,' Dakshina reassured her.

And Jodie would be inclined to agree. Only, her dream had already started but swiftly turned into her worst nightmare. And now she had to start all over again, only this time she was alone. Very much alone.

CHAPTER FOUR

HARPER

Gym. Sesh. On.

Knowing that six weeks with absolutely no contact between them would be too much of an adjustment, Harper and Jodie had agreed to message each other daily. Not the usual long messages or hour-long chinwags detailing every part of their lives. Instead, they were limited to three words or emojis to give an insight into what they were both up to and as a way of letting each other know they were okay.

It had been Harper's idea because she didn't want to have the usual lengthy conversations. Not because she suddenly didn't care about her sister, but she didn't want either of them to lose focus on establishing themselves in their new realities. Every minute they'd spend corresponding would stand in the way of her piecing back together the parts of her life that were still intact.

Since Harper had been moved to Stoke Mandeville Hospital for rehabilitation at the National Spinal Injuries Centre, she'd learnt an astonishing amount of things she needed to do to take good care of herself. Things that had previously been automatic now needed thought, care and attention. Having a circuit breaker in her autonomic nervous system was no minor issue, but she was surrounded by experts, from the consultants to the care assistants, and she was willing to learn. In her brief note to her sister, she'd only included what would be the highlight of the day: *Gym. Sesh. On.* Building her muscles up so she would get to a place where she'd be able to move herself around with ease. She didn't include things like learning to take care of her catheter bag, or the fact she was still struggling with centring her balance now her sensation had changed the dynamics. She didn't include the fact that none of this was easy. And she didn't like to admit that her three words idea had been so she didn't have her sister's daily life as a direct comparison. Right now, it would be more crushing than she was prepared to admit.

'What would you like to talk about today?' Yasmine, the psychologist, asked after she'd wheeled Harper with permission into a private consultation room.

She wouldn't be telling Jodie about this either. As part of her rehab, Monday through to Friday, she had a half-hour session with a psychologist.

'I thought you were supposed to guide the sessions and what we talked about?' Harper remarked. It was a bit like being advised to follow a diet. There were certain subjects that had to be covered as a necessity. She sensed it was so people would open up and bare their war wounds, but she preferred to keep herself as a closed book.

'Sometimes the scheduled sessions aren't for everyone. I thought you might like the chance to choose what we talk about today?'

A silence followed that Harper was unable to fill. There was plenty she could say, but would that really help?

'Okay, if not, I'll ask you some questions then?'

Harper glanced at Yasmine, noticing more about her with each session. She was in her thirties with long dark hair tied in a plait behind her back. There were no photos to indicate she had any family and nothing personal to give any nod to her life outside the hospital.

'What's your favourite colour?' Yasmine asked.

Harper moved her gaze to the door. Maybe it was time to start counting the minutes until she'd be able to leave. 'What is this? Start with the easy questions, work out if I'm being honest, then move on to the tricky stuff?'

'Nope. I just wanted to know your favourite colour.'

Harper shrugged. She might as well use the movement she still had, after all. 'If I was pushed to choose one it would be red, I guess.' She wasn't going to add that it had been the colour that distinguished her as being Harper all her life.

'And what was your favourite colour before the accident?'

She let out an exasperated sigh. She'd known before she'd answered that she was falling into a trap. She'd have been better off not saying anything.

'It was red, right?' Yasmine said.

'Do you want points for a correct answer?' Harper wouldn't usually talk to anyone like this, and she didn't like hearing herself.

'No, I just wanted to illustrate a point.'

'And what was that?'

'I wanted you to realise that some things haven't changed. That some of the things you liked before, you'll still like now. And some of the things you did before, you'll be able to do now. With others being in a different format. And you probably need to hear the fact that it's okay to be angry. It's natural, in fact.'

Harper knew what she was trying to do. Yasmine was trying to paint a pretty picture to help her accept her situation. But what she didn't seem to realise was that Harper would never be a painting. Not when she had a mirror image. One that could still get up and walk. She was static while her counterpart would always be moving.

'What if I don't want to talk? What if I don't want to analyse every change that's occurring because a taxi broke my back in two? What if I'm angry about talking and would really rather not dissect how my life's turned out? What if I just want to get on with it instead?' Harper realised as the words left her mouth that, yes, she was angry. Because she had every right to be. Anyone would be in her situation, but that didn't mean she wanted to dwell. Because dwelling meant admitting it was hard to accept.

'These sessions are an important part of your rehabilitation. Whether you want to face up to it or not, major changes have occurred in your life, and we need to make sure we deal with the psychological side of that as well as the physical. That's why these sessions are an integrated part of the programme here.'

If Harper were a volcano, this was the point at which she would erupt. The realisation that she was more scared than she wanted to admit was pushing her anger out into the open. That, along with the knowledge that she was choosing to separate herself from the one person she'd normally confide in, but couldn't without facing up to her every hurt.

Her anger, that she hadn't known was there until now, had become hot lava that she wanted to flow out of her so she would be left alone. No one, having been through what she'd been through, would want to sit around and have a cosy chat about it just so she could gain gym access. To her it seemed like an unnecessary cruelty, but faced with no choice, perhaps she would share the one thing that was eating her up inside.

'You know I'm an identical twin, right?'

'I was aware of that from your notes. She was with you at the time of your accident, I believe?'

It was posed as a question, but Harper knew that Yasmine already knew the answer. That really, she didn't need to say anything more, and if she did, she'd be falling into another trap. For a moment, Harper decided not to talk. She let the lava flow out of her without using words. She didn't want to admit to all the things that hurt; it would somehow feel like giving in. She didn't see the point in being angry over something she couldn't change, and yet here she was, seething all the same.

'Do you want to talk about your sister?' Yasmine ventured.

'No,' Harper said, more forcefully than she'd intended. 'Sorry, I didn't mean to sound harsh. I just... for the first time in my life I need to be *me*. Jodie has always been such an integral part of my existence. We've done everything together our whole lives. This is the first time I've had to do something just for me. And right now, I don't need to see or hear or think about her. Not because I don't care, but because it hurts. She gets to live the life we dreamt of, and I don't. So, I don't want to talk about Jodie. I want to talk about me, about Harper. I want to talk about what's *she's* doing and what *her* dreams are now things have changed.'

Harper had divulged a whole lot more about how she was feeling than she'd meant to. Clearly, Yasmine was well practised in the art of getting patients to reveal what was really bothering them.

'And what are those things?'

Harper let out a breath through her nose, which made her nostrils flare. She was a sulking dragon that didn't want to join in, but had to admit that now she was in for a penny, she might as well be in for a pound. 'I'm not entirely sure, but what I do know is that they're selfish. Everything I'm doing at the moment is for me because it has to be.'

'And are you comfortable with that feeling?'

'Comfortable?' More steam poured from her new dragon nose. 'It's the most uncomfortable thing in the world. I've never been apart from my sister, but life hasn't given us much choice. I need to be here to get myself as strong and prepared as I can now I only have two functioning limbs. She can't put her life or dreams on hold because of what happened to me.'

'And how does that make you feel?'

Feelings. Feelings. *Feelings*. It was all this woman wanted to know, and it made Harper want to punch a wall. What bloody use were feelings to her at the moment?

'Angry,' Harper said, realising that she really was. 'Angry because this isn't how things should be. Angry because I can't cope with seeing my sister walking around while I'm struggling to keep my upper body balanced when I'm not propped up in a chair. Angry because I don't want to be apart from her, but I can't see any other way to make it better.'

'You're the first identical twin I've had as a patient here.'

'Well, at least you know. If you do ever see me walking about, it won't give you cause to faint.' Harper wiped away a tear that had managed to wind its way down her cheek.

Because however hard she'd been working on putting on a brave face, it turned out that in a private room away from anyone who knew her, she did have feelings. And even though she didn't want to voice it, it hurt. What had happened really hurt and she had to work out how to move on from how she felt right now.

Because she couldn't face it one step at a time. What she was facing now was an entirely different ball game.

CHAPTER FIVE

JODIE

One. More. Show.

Jodie sighed at the untruth she was telling her sister. Harper didn't need to know that the show was actually an audition. That the show they'd been involved with had ended up being a big flop. There was a chance that Harper would be following the theatre news in the stage magazine they usually read, but Jodie had to assume she was concentrating on other things.

Besides, with a limit of three words or icons there wasn't much room to lie, as such. It was a case of not being able to tell the full story.

The usual confidence Jodie possessed for auditions had escaped her and it wasn't hard to work out why. Without Harper by her side, it was an entirely different experience. Without her sister working out where they needed to go, Jodie couldn't drift to these places on a cloud with Harper in the driving seat. She had to engage all her senses to make sure she got to where she needed to be. For the first time ever, as she made her way there, her knees were trembling.

This theatre was even further away from the West End than the Witlow had been. Now she was deeper into East London. But London was London and a theatre was a theatre. If she managed to get this gig, it would see her through to the New Year. Having something that would allow her time to re-evaluate would be better than nothing at all.

Dakshina wasn't there. She'd messaged to say she'd been offered a four-month contract with one of the biggest shows in the West End. Funny how she'd not told Jodie about *that* audition. Nor had anyone else Jodie knew, and several of them had now landed roles. Each of them out for themselves, it would seem. So there was no one she knew.

It was the first time she'd waited to go on stage with no one to share the nerves and anticipation with. There was a small group also waiting, but they were very much a group, not even offering a glance her way.

When she got on the stage, the spotlight trained on her, she tried her usual trick of pretending there wasn't an audience there. But it was harder when the audience of three were talking to her and asking her questions.

'What piece are you going to be doing for us?' one of them asked.

'The finale from *Gingerbread*.' Jodie had decided it would be best to do a piece that was fresh in her memory.

'Ah, not one that any of us will be familiar with. Interesting choice.'

Was that bad? Should she have gone with something more classic? Or a pantomime piece? She knew plenty of other parts that she could perform, but had opted for a safe choice in terms of remembering every move.

'When you're ready,' someone else said.

Jodie got into position and tried not to overthink what had been said. She wasn't about to change her mind now. She'd have to give it her all. Demonstrate that even though the show had been a flop, it didn't mean *she* was.

For the next five minutes, Jodie threw herself into the performance, only occasionally flitting back to the moment that had stopped her sleeping at night. She was trying her best to not keep returning to that memory, but her thought patterns had other ideas. With everything she did, it was there ready to demonstrate itself.

Harper flying through the air propelled by the strength and skill she'd been honing for years, only to be struck by a taxi driver who'd been steering corners as if he were a Formula One driver. The crunch. The certain fear that the outcome would result in a funeral she wouldn't ever be ready to face...

It took a shake of the head to switch from those thoughts and bring her back to the present. When she took her bow, she hoped they hadn't noticed.

'Great. Thanks. We'll let you know in the next day or two.'

Jodie paused for a second on stage, drawing in air to catch her breath. 'I deserve a chance.' She was about to declare that her sister nearly dying didn't mean she brought any kind of curse with her, but she shut herself up before she said anything more.

She fled then, not sure why she'd said anything. Perhaps it was because in the same way she'd relived that moment, she felt as if she were being judged by it. Everyone in the world of theatre would have heard about Harper's accident. And doing the piece from *Gingerbread* had been a clear indicator of what production she was from. It had been foolish to choose it, but it was too late now.

'Hang on!' one of the directors yelled.

Jodie paused, turning to face them again.

'Come back at the same time tomorrow. We'll get you to run some lines.'

'Right,' she said, not knowing what else to say. Part of her wanted to tell him not to take pity on her, but there was a chance he wasn't. Her options weren't plentiful at the moment and she was never going to join her parents in their campervan. Not that they'd asked. She didn't want to admit defeat, as that would be failure, and she wouldn't just be failing herself. She'd be failing her sister as well.

When she got back to the flat she and Harper had rented for the month, there was someone waiting outside her door. And it wasn't anyone she recognised.

'Can I help?'

'Are you Jodie or Harper?'

If he knew anything about what had happened over the past month, he'd know she wasn't Harper. 'Why are you asking? Who are you?'

'I'm here to evict you. Apparently you've gone over your tenancy and you've not paid enough rent to stay.'

'But I explained to the landlord what's happened! I've paid my half and said I'd get the rest sorted as soon as possible.' When Jodie had spoken to the man she only knew as Theo, he'd seemed happy with the arrangement. Yes, the rent was due, but she'd got the impression, given the circumstances, he was happy to wait.

'Boss says you've overstayed without paying and we've got someone else wants this place. It wasn't a rolling contract. You can't just decide to stay as well as not pay. Not as far as I'm concerned. You've got half an hour to gather your things and get out. If you're not gone, I'll be coming back with my friends.'

'Give me an hour. I need to pack my sister's things as well.'

'Half an hour. Because you didn't say *please*.' With that he left, leaving Jodie staring in his wake.

Because he didn't appear to be the kind of person she should be arguing with, Jodie wasn't about to protest.

It didn't take much effort to work her way around what was more or less a bedsit to gather everything they'd brought with them. The plan had never been to be there long term, and they hadn't fully unpacked. They'd hoped things would improve incrementally. That one show would lead to another and the roles themselves would become bigger and better.

As it stood, Jodie was getting kicked out with only a vague hope of getting a short-term part in a panto. Once she'd finished packing, she realised she had no idea where she was going, or what she was going to do.

The man was waiting outside the building, standing in the freezing cold as if nothing, not even temperatures close to zero, would penetrate his bulk. She handed the keys to him. It was only on doing so that she realised it might be a mistake. For all she knew he might have been a chancer wanting the place for himself, but there was something about him that meant business.

'I think you're the one who needs to work on your manners,' she snarled as she walked away, trying to remain as dignified as possible while wheeling two suitcases.

As soon as she was round the corner, she stopped. What was she supposed to do? She couldn't lug her sister's belongings, as well as her own, around London indefinitely, but she couldn't abandon them either.

She wheeled them into a side street so she was hidden away, and tried to make a plan. If she could find somewhere to stay tonight, perhaps her parents would pass by to collect the second case? It seemed doubtful, knowing that currently they were enjoying the delights of Norfolk. So far, they'd only returned because of Harper's accident. Not wanting to remain camped out in a hospital car park, they were using it as an excuse to explore other parts of the UK. That seemingly hadn't included London, so they only popped by at weekends to make sure Harper was okay, and now she was in another part of the country, Jodie didn't have a hope of seeing them. Apparently, Jodie didn't feature in the required welfare checks. They might help, but they were just as likely to tell her to put it in storage.

But rather than finding any solutions straightaway, Jodie had a little cry while pretending to be on her phone. A little voice was telling her that Harper would know what to do. She was the twin in charge of every situation they'd ever faced. And she couldn't call her to rescue her like she usually would. She desperately wanted to, but she needed to last at least a week before folding. Instead, she had to find her own way, and right now, that seemed impossible given that she was both homeless and unemployed.

Some big London dream this was turning into.

CHAPTER SIX

HARPER

Transfers. Transfers. Transfers.

Considering their communication was limited to three words or symbols, it was perhaps a waste of the day's message to use the same word three times, but Harper couldn't think what else to add. Not when transfers were her life at the moment.

Not the footballing kind, and it was hard to know if her sister would have any idea what she meant. Their limited communication meant clarifying such things was impossible.

The kind of transfer she meant was from bed to chair. Her new nemesis that she was practising on the recommendation of her physiotherapist. On her ward. In the gym. Repeat. Repeat. Repeat. And eventually practice would make perfect. That's what she had to hope.

Despite her good physical condition prior to the accident, she was having to learn every movement from scratch. Without the powerhouse muscles of her legs propelling her, what she was trying to achieve was far beyond her current upper body strength. Her arms had generally been concerned with delicate positioning, not moving her entire frame. The technicalities of getting herself upright then moving to her wheelchair, currently with the use of a transfer board, with only her arm strength to rely on, and her changed centre of balance to compensate for, were proving more of a challenge than she'd ever imagined. But she was determined to conquer the task even if she was making her hands red raw from trying.

After about the fiftieth attempt that day, the head physiotherapist, Aden, interrupted her efforts.

'I've got someone here to see you.'

Harper did her best not to let her annoyance show. She didn't have time for random visits if she was going to make the most of these six weeks.

'I've asked my family not to visit during the week,' she said. Hopefully he'd take the hint that if she wasn't seeing family, then she didn't want to meet anyone else.

'I like to buddy newbies up with mentors. People who've been here and got the T-shirt.'

The sound of chair wheels coming into the gym meant it was too late to protest.

'Harper, meet Maceo. Maceo, meet Harper.'

Maceo performed a series of moves in his slimline wheelchair, including hopping on one wheel as if he were performing a break dance. He was slick in every sense. Slick buzz cut, slick muscles, slick moves. Harper liked him instantly and imagined he had that effect on everyone he met. She couldn't help but be impressed and long for the day when she'd be able to perform such stunts. Once he'd finished, she realised she was staring. Who wouldn't be, given his broad black shoulders (he was wearing a basketball jersey that showed them off to full effect) that he must have spent hours working on?

'How you doing?' Maceo asked.

'Not *that* well,' she said, referring to his wheelchair antics.

'Believe me, that's taken practice. So, Aden tells me you've been going at it hardcore.'

Harper glanced to see where her physiotherapist was, but he'd cleverly merged into the corner of the gym as if he knew his presence wouldn't help.

'I just want to get to the point where it's easy. I thought that would come quicker than it has.'

'Show me your hands.'

'Pardon?'

'Show me your hands. That way I know whether you're overdoing it or not.'

Harper didn't want to, knowing there were telltale signs of the day's efforts. 'Why should I? What qualifies you to know best?'

Maceo held out his hands, which were covered by fingerless gloves. 'I promise this is not a case of mansplaining. I come to the gym every week and Aden thought it might be useful if I spoke to you. I learnt some of my lessons the hard way. He matches patients up to try and make those lessons a little easier.'

Taking his gloves off, Maceo showed her a red line that marked his palm. 'I managed to do this within seventy-two hours of arriving here. I was so determined to get to where I am now that I ended up damaging myself in the process. The wound on my hand got infected, and set me back by a couple of weeks. But it was a lesson I needed to learn. Sometimes you can't rush things. I think that might be the nugget of wisdom Aden was hoping I'd share with you.'

Realising she'd been defensive when she hadn't needed to, Harper turned her palms to show him. He was here as friend, not foe. She'd hoped the redness would have gone down slightly while he was talking but, if anything, it was more apparent.

'We need to make sure you get some decent gloves. And you need to rest. Nothing else that'll be heavy going on your palms for the rest of today.'

'It's just so frustrating.'

'It can be, but try to think about it like learning to drive. You have to take lessons before you can pass a driving test. But we don't learn when we're babies. We learn those skills later in life when we're able to. This is the same. We need to learn a new set of skills before we'll pass our test.'

Harper didn't want to point out that she'd never passed a driving test. She'd never had the confidence to continue beyond the set of ten lessons her parents had given her as a present.

'What happened for you to need a wheelchair? Only tell me if you're happy to.' She didn't want to pry, but she wanted to know why Aden had thought introducing them was a good idea.

'It was a rugby injury. An unusual one because often they're higher up. But here I am, T12 complete.'

Harper's injury was at the same level, meaning that their range of function would be identical. She'd not felt identical to anything recently, even though that had been her status for her entire life. 'Snap,' Harper said. 'Literally,' she added, drily.

Maceo creased into laughter, lines forming across his handsome face. 'Man, that hurts,' he remarked as he continued to laugh.

Harper found herself smiling. Anyone laughing that hard at her dry humour was worth knowing.

'Do I get to find out what caused yours?' he asked, once he'd got over his laughing fit.

'Stupidity,' she said, before realising he was looking at her seriously now and she wanted to tell the whole story. 'We were at the end of our first week's run of the show I was in and the whole cast decided to dance across the road. I decided to show off because I wanted to impress the director and I did a butterfly jump. It requires quite a lot of lift, and before I got my feet back on the ground I'd been hit by a black cab.'

'Shit. What a way to be taken out.' Maceo shook his head at

the unfairness of it all. Both of them in their early twenties, and both unable to do the things they loved.

'At least I was dancing when it happened. That makes me feel slightly better.'

'For a while, I wished I'd died. That the tackle had taken me out completely. Somehow it felt like being paralysed was more of a punishment than death. But then I realised I'm still Maceo. And nothing can get Maceo down!' He did a turn in his chair to prove the point.

Harper hadn't had those kinds of thoughts. Partly because she had a sister who would always depend on her. It was nice to be talking to someone who hadn't read her medical notes and wouldn't know she was a twin. And for now she was going to keep it to herself. She was just Harper. Alone. He didn't need to know yet.

'I'm glad to hear it,' she said, genuinely grateful he'd got past that point because here he was... a ray of gorgeous sunshine brightening the room. 'And what's Maceo doing now?'

'Training. Lots of training. Because it turns out you can still play rugby even if you don't have the use of your legs. I've joined the local wheelchair rugby team and eventually I'm hoping to join a league. I've got the Paralympics in my sights.' He flexed one of his guns and used his other arm to twirl himself in a circle. She wished she had that kind of finesse with her chair, but seeing it in action was making her realise it was possible. But patience was going to be key.

'I wonder...' Her words trailed off before she completed the sentence.

'What are you wondering?'

Harper shook her head, not wanting to say it out loud.

'You're among friends here.' Maceo checked there was no one else in earshot in the gym.

'I wonder if I'll ever dance again...' Given that she couldn't get herself from bed to chair or from chair to chair in an elegant manner at the moment, it seemed like an impossible dream. One for her last lifetime, not this one.

'Of course you will!' Maceo wheeled beside her. 'But today you need to let your hands rest.'

Harper glanced at her palms briefly and knew he was right. For some reason she'd not really been willing to listen to the medical professionals about overdoing it. As a dancer she'd been overdoing it all her life. But now, after talking to someone who'd been through the same process, listening seemed like a wise move.

'Don't look so crestfallen. It doesn't mean we can't exercise in other ways. How about I show you the best yoga moves from a wheelchair.'

'What? You mean you aren't just here to bulk up your muscle and show me your best moves?'

Maceo faked shock. 'What do you think of me? I can stretch like the best of them. This does mean you're agreeing to have a gym buddy, though. You know that?'

Harper shrugged. 'Beats talking to myself.'

'Nice to know I'm going to be appreciated.' Maceo grinned.

Over the next hour, Maceo patiently went over one of the yoga routines he did regularly. He explained the benefits of each manoeuvre and she tried not to let her gaze linger on his muscles for too long. She had a feeling he knew he was in good shape without her boosting his ego. Instead, she focussed on what they were doing as they both stretched muscles that were in need of it. Both the mobile and immobile ones.

By the time it was over, Harper was suitably exhausted. It turned out she didn't have to be fiercely trying to get from bed to chair with ease in order to wear herself out. And with less resistance than the lowest-grade exercise band available, she'd given Maceo her phone number when he'd asked for it. He only came once a week normally, but he'd offered to visit more frequently during her stay to be an official gym buddy on the days she needed motivation.

To her surprise, it had been a welcome development. Even though on the whole she was doing okay (angry therapy sessions aside), she was missing her sister. Her best friend who happened to have the same DNA. Her best friend with whom she no longer had a matching anatomy. And having a new friend, even an overly confident one with a megawatt smile, was better than facing this alone.

Because even though her thoughts hadn't reached a place as dark as Maceo's had, it didn't mean that this wasn't the scariest thing she'd ever gone through.

If the injury itself wasn't enough to adjust to, not having her sister by her side was far worse.

CHAPTER SEVEN

JODIE

Take. A. Bow.

The phrase 'fortune favours the brave' had been popping into Jodie's head every day this week. Because currently she should be on her knees, but somehow she was still upright.

When she'd spoken to her parents about Harper's belongings, they'd agreed to pay for them to go into storage temporarily, claiming there was no available space in their van. They'd moved from Norfolk to the Kent coast now, having ducked by to visit her sister. Not her. Their avoidance wasn't hard to spot. They'd always been hands-off, but she sensed there was an element of blame, not that she'd seen them for long enough to know whether that was true. Mostly, her parents weren't giving up their selfish streak and planned to continue travelling, whatever the circumstances.

On the way to her second audition, Jodie had decided she didn't care how big or small the part was, she just needed to land a role to get her through the Christmas period. She didn't want Harper to come out of six weeks of rehabilitation to find her unemployed and not living the dream like she'd promised she would be. And even if the dream came as playing the part of Santa's elf, if it was on stage, then at this point it counted.

It was a huge relief when they rang to say she'd landed a role. She was going to be part of the chorus, but she was also the understudy for the part of Goldilocks. There was a chance, if the lead needed any time off or was sick, that she'd end up playing the main character. Despite it being a small theatre in the East End, the thought sent a frisson of excitement to her stomach.

Unfortunately, that frisson couldn't be used as payment for a roof over her head. Having managed to stay with Dakshina for one night, it had been made very clear by her parents that it was a one-off and wasn't a long-term solution. So for the second night in a row, she was staying at a hostel. It had cost her less than one hundred pounds to book for six nights, including a basic breakfast. The downside was that she was in a dorm room with up to seven other people. At first, she'd wondered if this was what prison felt like, only she doubted that prisons had passing hen parties waking everyone at ungodly hours.

'What's your story, then?' It was the dorm-mate who appeared to be a permanent fixture. She'd observed Jodie's every move since she'd arrived. She was obviously here on a more long-term basis. She had the bottom bunk in the bed nearest the window and she'd fashioned a curtain round the edges with what appeared to be a sarong and a towel.

'What do you mean?' Jodie asked, having returned from another late rehearsal.

'Why are you here?' The girl, who must have been a similar age, wasn't coming across as super friendly.

'To sleep. I just needed a place to stay for a few nights. Sorry, I didn't catch your name?'

'That's because I didn't give it to you. When you leaving?'

'Wow. Do you make many friends talking to people like that?'

'I'm not here to make friends, bitch.'

'Great, well, don't worry yourself. I'm not planning on becoming a permanent resident.'

Thankfully that ended any further discussion, but as Jodie got ready for bed she had to admit to herself that she wasn't at all comfortable spending the night in a room with someone that hostile. Even having a hen party in here with them like they had the previous night would be preferable. Or if her roommate had continued her silent brooding, rather than declaring her hatred of others sharing the room.

Jodie returned from the bathroom to find the girl hidden behind her makeshift curtains. She settled into her bed and wondered if she needed to say a prayer about making it to the morning. As soon as her head hit the pillow, the music started. Not loud enough for the other rooms to hear, but a steady stream of heavy metal. It would seem the campaign to get Jodie out had begun in the most passive-aggressive way possible.

Four. More. Nights.

Perhaps that's the message she could send her sister next. A countdown of how many days she was going to be subjected to this torture aimed at preventing her from sleeping. Only perhaps not. She didn't want Harper thinking that anything was less than perfect. And she tried not to cry into her pillow as she thought about how her life was taking one step forwards and two steps back. At least she could take steps. She wasn't the one with the raw deal, even if trying to fall asleep to the sounds of Alice Cooper was the last thing she needed right now. There was a roof over her head. She had food in her belly. She'd got a part in another production. So why did she feel so lost?

She. Missed. Harper.

It was that simple. She knew it hadn't been long, but she already doubted she would be able to go a whole six weeks without seeing her sister. It wasn't like she was able to turn to their parents. She knew she needed to find her own place in the world, but that didn't stop her missing her sister and wanting her there to navigate the way for her like she usually did. One thing was certain... staying in this hostel wasn't helping.

CHAPTER EIGHT

HARPER

Patience. IsA. Virtue.

Harper had not long dipped her hands in a wax bath, and the soft skin of wax was hardening on her like a pair of gloves. It wasn't something she'd ever heard of, but Aden had suggested it as it was often used as treatment for arthritis and joint pains. She didn't have any open wounds, only some redness, so he'd suggested it would help with giving her hands some respite.

Anything that would speed up her recovery was going to receive a yes from her, but now she wondered if it was just a way to make her stay still for a while. The wax needed to remain in place for twenty minutes and she wouldn't be able to remove it until it had solidified. It was the closest she'd come to a beauty treatment for a while.

'I always knew Aden was a genius,' Maceo commented when he arrived and saw her temporarily incapacitated.

'Trust you to be on his side.' Harper stuck her tongue out, making good use of the parts of her body she could move.

Maceo laughed, and it seemed to fill the whole room with

joy, a laugh as large as his stature. She'd have marked him as a
basketball player if she hadn't known any better. Even though
they were both in chairs, he still towered over her. Harper
wished she could hold on to that laugh, so it could keep her
company in the middle of the night. Instead, she was just
thankful it was here now. She'd been thankful every time he'd
arrived with his brooding dark brown eyes. She was trying not
to fall into his lingering glances – she didn't need that distraction. Instead, she was getting used to his swagger, appreciating
the fact it could have easily been lost, but here it was, as bold as
the sun.

'Any chance I can dip my palms as well?' Maceo asked
Aden.

'Go ahead! Make use of it while it's on,' Aden said,
returning to another patient.

Maceo dipped his hands in the hot wax.

'This isn't your first rodeo, then?'

'Not at all. I did this almost daily when I was an inpatient.
Made them turn the machine on especially for me. Can you do
the honours, Aden?'

Aden wheeled Maceo over to Harper as the wax gloves
prevented him from spinning himself like he usually would.

'How are your hands doing? Have you rested them like I
suggested?' Maceo asked.

Harper gestured a Girl Guide's promise, although not with
much finesse given that her fingers were beginning to weld
together. 'There's just some redness now, and I have proper
gloves to use for when I get started again.'

'These ones won't help you that much.' Maceo waved his
waxed hands. 'Although they do make your skin as soft as a
baby's bottom. Cheers for letting me join in, Aden.'

'No worries,' the physio said, before heading away to help
some of his other patients – a regular crowd of inpatients and
outpatients. Some were at the beginning of their journey, like

Harper, and some were a couple of years on, like Maceo. Aden was in the habit of pairing patients up with a mentor, so all around the gym there were pairs of patients working out. A week on and Harper was beginning to settle into this newfound friendship.

'Have you ever had this treatment before?' Maceo asked.

'Nope. This is my first time.'

'Ah, so you don't know that this isn't even the best bit.'

Relaxing with her hands covered in a substance that was making them feel like they had one of those lovely heated face masks on definitely seemed to be a best part. 'What do you mean?' she asked.

'You'll see. Let's relax until the timer goes off.'

Harper wasn't going to argue. She'd not been resting enough, she knew that. Her body had been in a state of tension ever since the accident. At the time, she'd thought she was a goner. And that sense of an ending seemed to have remained, leaving her muscles rigid or non-compliant, despite Harper wanting to move on to the next stage. She'd been pushing herself as much as humanly possible, like she had with her dance training. So even if it was only for twenty minutes, it was nice to take some time out from focussing on all the things she wanted to be able to do, but couldn't yet manage.

When the timer went off, Harper looked at Maceo. 'What do we do now, then?'

'Now for the fun part,' he said, as he started pulling the wax off.

It was like pulling off a hardened face mask, only one that was much thicker and could be moulded into shapes, as Maceo demonstrated. It wasn't a particularly quick task, but surprisingly therapeutic.

'Feel my palm.' Maceo offered his hand. It shone from the treatment.

Harper ran a finger across his lifeline and it seemed to send a shiver through him.

'Like a baby's bottom, right?'

'How about mine?' Harper offered her shiny palm.

Maceo did the same, and a shiver went through her, as if electricity had passed through her body. Even the parts she couldn't feel, like a ghost trailing along the skin where the neurons weren't sparking like they once had.

'Beautiful. And you're going to live a long and happy life,' he said, once he'd finished tracing her lifeline.

'How can you tell?'

His eyes hadn't left hers, and if they weren't in a sweaty hospital gym it might have been the kind of moment that could be considered romantic. She knew at some point he'd have her in his spell, and she was surprised to find she didn't mind that, but instantly dismissed the notion. She was here for rehabilitation. Nothing else.

Maceo shrugged. 'I have a sense for these things. Call it intuition.'

Still, he held her gaze and she was almost fully mesmerised, but she broke off the interaction by staring at her palms again. Because however hard Maceo stared at her, she wasn't going to fall for it as she was sure many girls had before. They were gym buddies. They were helping each other out on a short-term basis. She had six short weeks to go through before she'd be reunited with her sister.

One week down.

Five to go.

And, yes, she was counting.

CHAPTER NINE

JODIE

Nine to five.

'Do you have any experience?' The café owner looked Jodie up and down, taking in her slender frame. Judgements on her aesthetics were clearly part of the interview.

'I did the lunch shift at my student union once a week, when I was at university studying dance and drama.'

'Was it busy?'

Jodie wasn't sure what classified as busy. They'd had more visitors than this place currently did, but she didn't know how to word that without being insulting. 'Yes, most of the time it was.'

'When can you start?'

'Tomorrow.'

'Stay and do a one-hour trial today, and if you do okay, the job's yours.'

'Okay, great,' she said through gritted teeth.

She wondered how many one-hour trials this guy had conducted in order to cover his lunch shifts. But what choice did she have? If she didn't do this trial, she definitely wouldn't have a job tomorrow and she needed the extra income desperately. Nowhere was as cheap as the hostel she'd been staying in, but she'd had to leave, the hostile roommate depriving her of sleep at every opportunity.

She'd booked a few nights in a room above a pub and it was eating away at her funds, but she had her own space and wasn't worried about sharing with any weirdos. She was sharing a bathroom, but as it was cleaned daily, it hadn't been too horrendous so far. But the costs were mounting. So the next hour was important. There weren't many places taking on staff for lunchtimes only. Most of them wanted staff for the evenings and weekends as well, which was when she was busy in the not especially well-paid panto land.

The café owner, Vince, went through some brief explanations of what Jodie needed to do for her trial. There wasn't a modern system in place, so orders were taken down on paper before being passed to the chef, Antoine, and any maths was carried out on a calculator before being put through the till. All orders were duplicated so the owner could tally the takings with the till at the end of the day. It all made sense to Jodie and the hour went relatively quickly with a steady stream of customers – never enough to cause a queue, but plenty to keep her busy.

When the hour was up, the owner didn't give any sign that she was permitted to leave. One hour of free labour was all she was willing to give, though. It was a gamble she'd been willing to take, but he wasn't going to get any more time from her unless it was paid.

He'd been working on his laptop, making out he was busy sorting orders and logging the takings, but she knew he was keeping an eye on her. Taking off the apron she'd been provided with, she placed it on the table he was sitting at so he would know she was done.

'Same time tomorrow?' she asked.

'You're honest, yes?'

'Yes,' she remarked, realising that anyone dishonest would say the same.

'Tomorrow. Same time.'

'Great. See you then.'

It was a relief to have something extra in place given that she wouldn't be able to remain in London past Christmas without improving her income. She needed to find a more permanent solution to her accommodation problem, but at the moment she was thankful for a room of her own, however much it was adding to her expenses. She slipped back to the pub and had a shower to wash off the grease from the café and prepare herself for the big night.

Because rehearsals were over. Today was opening night for the pantomime. She should be more excited, but she couldn't help reflecting on what the dream had looked like when she and Harper had arrived in London, and what that dream was now.

They certainly didn't look the same when held up to the light.

CHAPTER TEN

HARPER

Whole. New. World.

Harper found she now enjoyed the therapy sessions that were a requirement of her stay. At first she'd sat there with a ball of anger, but now she was past that stage, the conversations she had with Yasmine were increasingly pleasant.

One of the things she was enjoying was asking all the awkward questions. It might be a cruel kind of enjoyment, but every time she made Yasmine blush she gave herself a point on an imaginary scoreboard.

'So, how do I have sex in the future? What does that look like?'

The blush was there in nanoseconds.

It was a valid question, and she hadn't asked just to make the colour in Yasmine's cheeks rise. She was genuinely curious, especially as every time Maceo glanced at her she felt as if she were being undressed by his eyes. She was beginning to think he had that effect on everyone. Even Aden. And while she wasn't planning on doing anything with Maceo, she was still curious. These were things she needed to know for the future.

'Your sexuality won't change because of your injury. You'll still want to explore and enjoy sex with your partner. Like anyone's sex life, it'll take exploration and working out what works. Libido won't be affected necessarily, and you can still get pregnant so you'd need to take precautions. What do you think it'll look like?'

It was Harper's turn to blush. She didn't want to voice the fact that she'd been wondering if she'd ever be able to with Maceo. She wasn't sure where to start.

'And if you just so happened to both be paraplegic, the same answer stands. You'd work it out.' Yasmine said it with a knowing smile on her face.

Damn having a psychologist who was observant enough to know what she was really asking.

'So, how are you feeling about forming relationships? Now or in the future?'

Harper felt her blush deepening, and she knew if she had marshmallows, she'd be able to toast them with the heat radiating from her cheeks. 'I'm not really thinking about it currently.'

'Really? Your question indicates that perhaps you are.'

Yasmine allowed the statement to linger between them. Oh, she was good.

'I've only been hypothesising in my mind. Working out what it would look like. Currently, I want to focus on getting myself stronger. I want to get to the point that I'm independent again and not reliant on anyone else for help.'

'That doesn't mean you can't think about what new relationships might exist in your life.'

'Exactly. I've been *thinking* about it. That doesn't mean I'm acting on anything. Or doing anything. Just mentally preparing for the future.'

Athletes often sacrificed parts of their lives to achieve their goals. Right now, she was an athlete after the gold. Even if that gold was only hypothetical. It was a stage of her life she was desperate to meet. Nothing, not even Maceo, was going to get in the way of that. Not when he was supposed to be part of the solution. 'I just don't feel able to at the moment. I mean, I know I've asked you about how my sex life might look, but I need to be stronger in every sense before I even think about that.'

'Mental preparation can be a healthy thing. That's why we tend to forecast our lives. We need to be ready for things to come. You just need to make sure the balance is right. Sometimes we can focus on certain details so intently that we forget to look at the big picture. Just make sure you take the time to appreciate the complete view.'

Harper wondered if Yasmine realised that as well as being her gym buddy, Maceo was sometimes a distraction. Right now, her priority was learning to transfer without needing someone nearby. Nothing else mattered. She'd thought she would have perfected it by now, but the sore hands she'd developed from overdoing things had held her back. She was back to practising regularly again, and doing regular weights in the gym, but something that should be simple was still proving problematic.

'I'll bear that in mind,' Harper said, not sure what else to say.

'How's your sister? Has she been in touch?'

Ah, here was Yasmine taking charge of the session again, undeterred by Harper's curveball questions. 'We vowed to just send each other three words or symbols a day. It's to help me concentrate on my rehab.'

'That's an interesting concept. Whose idea was that?'

She wasn't sure what Yasmine would make of the fact that it had been hers, but as she wasn't about to get detention for revealing it, she decided telling her wouldn't hurt.

'It was mine. I wanted to give Jodie permission to continue her life without me.'

'Are you giving yourself the same permission?'

This always happened. She would come in wanting to be in charge of the session, asking Yasmine the awkward questions, only for Yasmine to expertly turn the tables. 'I guess I must be.'

'And is it the reason you're so determined to be better?'

There was no fooling Yasmine, however hard she tried. It didn't take much contemplation to give her answer.

'Yes. My twin sister witnessed me in the worst kind of accident. She saw me broken, and I could see it was breaking her at the same time. In the time that she could visit, the tiredness was seeping out of her. I didn't want her to stretch herself for me, and I didn't want to see the sorrow in her eyes, so I suggested a break. That way, next time we see each other, she won't have to feel sorry for me. She'll be proud because what's happened hasn't defined me. Or her.'

'Did you talk to your sister about how she feels?'

Harper had to think. Had she? They'd talked about how recovery was going and how the show was going, but had they ever talked about how they were both feeling in the aftermath? It had been a raw wound lying between them, one that neither of them were prepared to explore, scared to find out how bad it really was.

'Not really. I guess everything happened so quickly, and when I came here we'd already made the decision to have this system in place. It seemed sensible to have some time apart to adjust. We've been in each other's pockets since we were babies. We've never really been apart. A break seemed necessary in the circumstances.'

'And do you think three words a day is adequate? Don't you want to call your sister and have a proper catch-up? Discuss how you're both feeling?'

There was nothing stopping that from happening. It wasn't

like anything would change if they didn't stick to the system they'd set out.

'Yes, I do. I can't tell you how many times I've picked up my phone and almost called her without thinking. But then I remember... I don't want to know about the life I would have been living. No one else here has that. A life being lived in parallel. The one that would have existed. And I just need to feel stronger, that's all. I need to learn to be Harper without Jodie at my side. Besides, six weeks isn't so long. We're already a third of the way through. It's working for now.'

So far it had been a bit like sticking to a diet. Every day she managed to keep at it felt like a triumph. It meant she was closer to her goal and it wasn't forever. It was temporary. In four weeks they'd be able to get together and discuss how things were. Their reunion wasn't so far away.

'Have you spoken to Maceo about this?'

Harper looked up sharply, almost giving herself whiplash. The question shouldn't have been surprising, but it made her panic. 'He doesn't know. You wouldn't tell him, would you?'

'Everything you tell me here is confidential. As is all your medical information. I just wondered if you'd spoken to anyone about it, given that you haven't spoken to your sister.'

During her sessions with Yasmine, Harper always found herself switching between wanting to divulge everything, and not wanting to say anything for fear of what Yasmine would think or add to her notes. Who didn't tell their friend that they had an identical twin sister?

'He doesn't even know I have a sister.'

'And why have you opted not to share that with him?'

'I wish I knew,' Harper said, letting out a humourless laugh.

'You must have your reasons.'

It didn't take long for Harper to work it out. 'I didn't want him to know there's an identical living, breathing, *walking* version of myself that exists.'

'And why's that, do you think? What's the reason for not wanting him to know?'

'Because I don't want him to want to meet her so he can draw comparisons. I've had enough of that in my life.'

'Do you really think he'd do that?'

'Maybe not. I also wanted to have something to myself for a while. Being a twin means you share so many things. Even our parents got us joint birthday cakes. What kid only gets half a birthday cake? For once, I figured I'd keep that fact to myself. I've never really been able to, so I decided I would. I didn't really consider the reasons why at the time.'

Harper stopped talking, realising she hadn't kept anything to herself at all. The truth was, she was finding these therapy sessions useful. She'd been through a significant trauma, and not being with her sister meant she didn't have her usual source of support. Being able to speak to Yasmine was helpful, even if sometimes she was left with more questions than answers. She might know that sex was still on the agenda in the future, but she was left wondering whether she should talk to her sister, and whether keeping her sibling a secret from Maceo was a good idea.

Far too many things in her life felt like the answer to her first question... it was exploratory. Sometimes it was a case of finding out what worked because the answers wouldn't be the same for everyone. They might not even be the same answers every day of the week.

For now, three words a day was a comfort without having to answer any of the big questions. And for now, that suited Harper just fine. If only her therapy sessions weren't making her question if that was really true...

CHAPTER ELEVEN

JODIE

Morning. Please. Thankyou.

Jodie pressed send on her message and had no idea what her sister would make of it. It was a list of some of the phrases her new boss didn't seem capable of saying. Oh, he was as nice as pie to the customers, just not so much to his employees.

For a moment, Jodie imagined what Harper would make of it if she were still by her side. She was pretty certain her sister would have said something, being the more forthright of the two. Rudeness was one of the things she'd never put up with. But Jodie wasn't Harper, she reminded herself, and this was to make ends meet.

Every day that Jodie went into the café she had to remind herself it was only for three hours. At least five times during those three hours she'd consider that they were hours of her life she'd never get back. Hours that could be spent doing other things with politer people.

The saving grace was Antoine, the chef. He wasn't much taller than her, slim and originally from Greece. Some days his hair was as slick as the oil in the fryers, but unlike Vince, their boss, he didn't leave his manners at home. And it was fortunate that she spent most of those three hours in his company, with Vince liking to be at his laptop or chatting to the customers, or nowhere to be seen.

Today there'd been a particularly turbulent start to the day, with a customer complaining that their food was too hot. This was a new type of complaint for Jodie. Surely that was the preferable state for the food to be in? Weren't most people taught as children to check the temperature of their food? It wouldn't have been a problem if they'd waited a couple of minutes. She figured there was no pleasing some people. And customer complaints never seemed to please Vince, even when the customer was being unreasonable.

'We can't have customers burning their mouths!' he'd shouted at Antoine.

'What do you expect me to do? Serve hot food with ice cubes, just in case? Isn't it commonplace for humans to check the temperature of their food before ploughing it into their mouths?'

Antoine usually took the telling-offs with a bowed head and determined grace. But not today. Given that he'd not done anything wrong, Jodie didn't blame him. Vince told him how disrespectful he was and stomped off.

Jodie had wondered if he did it for the drama, almost like he was putting on a show for the customers. As if, somehow, shouting and throwing his arms in wild gestures at his staff while remaining polite to everyone else would gain him custom. Oddly, it seemed to be working. There were regulars who came into the café every day and others who would frequent on the same day each week, and they seemed to enjoy the drama. It was as if they lived for the gossip they gained here. That and Antoine's *hot* cooking.

'You think he'd side with us on occasion, wouldn't you?'

Jodie said to Antoine now the coast was clear of both Vince and lunchtime customers.

'Oh no! Vince lives by the saying "the customer is always right". Even when the customer is a rude imbecile. It's tiresome.'

'Why do you put up with it?' As far as Jodie knew, Antoine had worked at the café for years. It was a long time to put up with being berated so frequently, and never having Vince on his side.

'Because it pays the bills and I'm doing what I love. Believe me, if I had the money to open my own place I would do it, no question. But London is expensive, you know this. That's why you're here.'

Jodie plonked her elbows on the counter and rested her head in her hands. She wasn't allowed to do it when Vince was there. Apparently it made her look lazy. That might be why she enjoyed doing it so much.

'Sooo expensive,' she sighed.

'Still looking for somewhere?'

Jodie had discussed her living situation with Antoine at length. He had a place in a house share, but the landlord had strict rules about who was able to stay, so he'd not been able to offer Jodie a room. He'd moved various times since arriving in London, sometimes being turfed out at short notice, or hit with unmanageable rent rises. He wasn't the least bit surprised by her landlord sending a heavy around to send her packing.

The pub that she was staying above was in no way a long-term solution. It was eating up all her wages and there wasn't much left. One of the perks of the café job, and one of the reasons she was putting up with Vince's attitude, was that she was sent away with a lunch each day. Okay, it was whatever happened to be left over, but as she walked from the café to the theatre, she had something to keep her going that hadn't added to her expenses. She finished at the café at three and had to be at the theatre by five, ready to do her make-up and get prepared for the evening show. The walk took about an hour, and when the weather was nice, she stopped in the park to eat her free lunch.

Today, it was pesto pasta. It wasn't her favourite, but as carb loading before a performance went, it was just the ticket. Really, it was a perfect moment. The skies were clear blue with the chill of winter in the air. Pigeons and grey squirrels kept watch to see if she'd be dropping any crumbs today. There was a steady stream of people passing through the park that were enough to indicate she was in London, but not so much that it was hectic. She had two jobs and somewhere to stay, at least for the moment.

It didn't stop her feeling like a dot on the planet, though. One that would look like an ant in the park if someone were to glance down from a plane window. And she wasn't sure how anyone could make their mark if they were only ever a dot. Two dots would always make more of a mark.

The thought that her sister should be beside her made her heart pang. An actual physical pain as if there were a handle on her chest that someone had tugged on. She was trying, but she didn't think she'd ever get used to Harper not being around. But she had to carry on.

Another night at the theatre. Another night of singing what she considered to be particularly bad versions of some popular Christmas carols. Another night of wanting to be reunited with her sister, but not wanting to disappoint her. And as she sat in a park between jobs, she considered exactly how close to the definition of disappointment she was right now.

Very, she thought.

CHAPTER TWELVE

HARPER

A different perspective.

It had been such a long time since Harper had been outside that she'd almost forgotten what it felt like. After training daily and with Maceo joining her at least three times a week, this had been his suggestion.

The cool breeze on her skin was such a welcome sensation that she wished she could take hold of it. Instead, she raised her hand into the air and let the wind lick invisible brushes between her fingers. The temperatures had dipped in the time since she'd become an inpatient and she was glad she'd wrapped up for the occasion.

The trip had been Maceo's idea. She sensed he probably hadn't expected Aden to join them, but Harper wasn't complaining. Having a gooseberry with them was welcome. It meant she could enjoy being with Maceo without having to worry about whether this constituted a date. She did not want to be on a date. She wasn't far enough along her journey to be considering such things.

Thankfully, she was far enough along her journey to have finally conquered transfers in all their varieties. She could transfer on the same level. She could transfer when there was a gap. She could transfer when it required her to go up from a lower level. It had taken much longer than she'd anticipated, given her fitness levels, and perhaps her own expectations of herself, but it had made it all the sweeter when she'd finally got there.

So a trip out like this one hadn't been as daunting as it would have been a couple of weeks ago. That achievement equalled being able to slip into the passenger seat of a taxi with her chair going in the boot with no problems.

Maceo had met them at the nature reserve, having driven himself with the use of a hand-controlled car. He looked more than a little deflated that she hadn't turned up alone, but Aden beat her to the explanation that she was still an inpatient and that this was being treated as a therapy session.

Despite whatever Maceo had been hoping, Harper was embracing being back in nature. Oddly, it wasn't an environment she hung out in that much. She could never be described as outdoorsy because she'd spent so many hours of her life in a dance studio. Several lessons in a day was the norm. Evenings and weekends spent perfecting moves, but never outside. Not until the night she got run over by a taxi, of course.

'There's a path we can follow that goes all the way around the lake,' Maceo said. 'It's wheelchair friendly, or we can go in a two-man canoe if you fancy?'

Harper didn't fancy. Not in any sense. Although, who was she trying to fool? The psychotherapist in her head? Maybe she could admit to herself that she did fancy him a little, but she wouldn't give in to it. And with each passing day she wondered if Maceo realised she was trying to resist his lilt and charm.

'Nah. Not a chance. The path around the lake it is.'

She may have mastered moving herself from one place to

another, but she wasn't about to test what her swimming looked like now she only had the use of her arms. When she did, it wasn't going to be in a cold lake in December. Not with the layers she had on.

By the time they were halfway round, Harper's upper arms were burning. She'd not realised how far it was. The fact she was able to see the other side when they'd started out had been deceiving. Because it wasn't the width of the lake she needed to worry about. It was the length. When they'd reached the other side, Harper reckoned she must have covered over a mile already, with Maceo leading the way and Aden trailing behind.

'Can we take a break?' she asked.

Maceo spun round to face her, smiling. 'But of course.'

'Did you know how far this was? You know I haven't done anything like this distance.'

'I knew how far. And so did your physio here. In fact, it was his suggestion.'

Harper glanced at Aden, who was a few paces behind. She sighed with relief that it was her physio and not Maceo suggesting potentially romantic locations.

'Was this your idea, Aden?'

''Fraid so,' he said, resting on a nearby fallen trunk. 'I haven't been here since Maceo was an inpatient and he was desperate to get some fresh air. I'd forgotten how much of a stretch this was.'

There was an option of asking Aden to push her the rest of the way. It was tempting, seeing as they were here because of him, but there was also a determination growing inside her. This was exactly the kind of thing she wanted to be doing. She needed to build herself up, and managing the other half of this trek would do exactly that. She promised herself some chocolate once they were done.

'I'm going to get going again. You two can catch me up,' Aden said.

Harper caught a movement out of the corner of her eye, and guessed it was Maceo making hand gestures to Aden. Great. He wanted to get her by herself. How did she get out of this one? At least there was a healthcare professional close by.

'Harper. Harper, Harper, Harper,' Maceo said in that singsong way of his.

'Yes?'

'Are you going to tell me what's up?'

'Why do you think something's up?'

'Look, I know we've only known each other a couple of weeks, but in that time I've come to know you. Have you ever heard of a tell?'

'A what?'

'A tell?'

'Nope.'

'I think it's a poker term. It's when a player acts in a way that somehow demonstrates whether they have a good hand or not. Sometimes it's a slight facial twitch or rubbing their knuckles. I don't think you realise, but whenever you're worried about something you rub your thumb on your nose. You were doing it a minute ago. So, tell me, what's stressing you out?'

What *wasn't* stressing Harper out would have been an easier question to answer. She'd been expecting a chat-up line, so being told he could tell when she was stressed surprised her.

'Is it being here with me?'

'No!' The word burst out of Harper with more vigour than she'd intended. She didn't want him thinking she didn't like him. Not that she wanted him to know that she *did* either.

'So, what is it?'

'I don't know.' She did really, but how to put it into words?

'Maybe you have some idea?'

This was beginning to feel a bit like a therapy session with Yasmine. He clearly knew her far too well already.

Harper caught herself rubbing her nose again. She snatched

her hand away, annoyed that her subconscious was so willing to give the game away. But in that moment she didn't know why she hadn't told him. It seemed... pointless, even though at the time it had seemed important.

'Tell me about your family, Maceo. Tell me about your parents and your siblings and how they've helped you through this.'

'Okay,' he said, before going on to give a rundown of his entire family tree.

His mum and dad were from Trinidad and had come to the UK soon after getting married. He was the youngest of four and was treated like the baby of the family. His sister, who was a lawyer and the only sibling other than himself who didn't have children, had converted an annex at her house to make it wheelchair accessible, and that was where he now lived. Harper should have asked Maceo before, but she'd been trying so hard to avoid talking about her sister that she'd deliberately swerved the subject.

'What about you? Tell me about your family.'

Harper switched her position in her wheelchair, as if making herself more comfortable would make talking about it easier. 'I should have said something sooner, but if I'm honest, I didn't want to.'

'Go on. No judgements here.'

'The thing is... I have an identical twin sister. Her name's Jodie. And when I say identical, I mean in *every* sense. We've done everything together our entire lives to the extent that we trained as dancers together and gained the same first job at the same time in London. We've always been together right up until I had the accident.'

'Why didn't you want to tell me? Having a twin must be cool.'

Harper placed her hands on the wheels of her chair. Not with the intention of moving, but to avoid rubbing her nose.

'This is going to sound a bit silly, but it was because I didn't want you to ask to meet her. I didn't want someone who's my friend in this new scenario to immediately request to meet the walking version of me. I didn't want comparisons to be drawn.'

'If I ever wanted to meet her, it would be because she's your sister. Not because I was going to play spot the difference. But this raises the question, why haven't I seen her? Surely she's been visiting?'

'I asked her not to. She was struggling with tiredness when she was coming to see me in hospital in London. I knew once I was transferred out here, travelling and continuing working in the show would be too much for her. So, I set her free. Or in less fancy terms, I told her she had to carry on living the dream we'd set out to achieve. I might not be able to do what we'd always wanted to, but that shouldn't stop Jodie. That's the last thing I'd ever want.'

'You sound like you feel guilty about that. Do you? Or am I imagining it?'

'There's a strong chance I feel guilty about everything. I feel guilty about not telling you. I feel guilty because she's on her own in London and that was never the plan, and I feel guilty about limiting our contact.'

'You're not keeping in touch?'

'We are. But only three words a day in texts. It only ever provides a snippet of information and some days it doesn't feel like enough, but I don't want to burden her with whatever crap I'm going through. I want her to concentrate on the life I was supposed to live.'

'Is that how it feels? That she's living the life you should have had?'

There was that guilt again. Feeling bad about everything that had occurred since the moment she flew through the air and ended up like a fly obliterated by a windscreen.

'I'm not jealous,' she was quick to say. 'I just want to get myself strong enough to not feel like I've failed when I'm next to her. I don't want to compare my life to hers and come up wanting. I want to find success in my own new way.'

Having held on to the fact she had an identical twin for a few weeks, it came as a relief to finally talk about Jodie to someone other than Yasmine, and without the fear that whatever she said would go on her medical record as part of her psychological evaluation.

'You will. I'm certain of it. But don't let any of those things get in the way of reaching out to her if you need to. My brothers and sister were rocks for me as I recovered. I don't mind telling you I had some very dark days. Times when I thought I'd be better off dead. My siblings were the ones who convinced me otherwise. Promise me that whatever agreement you have with your sister, you'll break it if you need to?'

'There's only three weeks left. If we've made it halfway, we should be able to manage the rest.'

'A lot can happen in three weeks. You need to be open to contacting her sooner. I can tell you're missing her.'

'I am. Constantly. But at the same time I know that being apart isn't doing either of us any harm. We both need to work out how to read our own compasses now we haven't got the other one to help guide the way.'

'You've obviously thought about it a lot.'

Harper wasn't sure she'd thought of much else. At least now she'd come clean, he'd know why she was so distracted. If concentrating on her own recovery wasn't enough, she was also concerned about how her sister was coping from afar. A deliberate afar. Because they were both having to unfurl from each other and spread their wings. And while being physically apart was hard, the emotional side of not having her person there all the time was much harder.

'Too much. Look, I'm glad I've told you. Now it's time to race round this lake.'

Harper didn't stop to hear his reply. She was too busy ensuring that the wind took her tears before he could see them. Confessing that she was missing her sister was enough without letting him know how much it hurt to not be with her, knowing it was her own selfishness that had enforced their separation.

CHAPTER THIRTEEN

JODIE

Curtains Up! Again.

Even though she wasn't communicating fully with Harper, Jodie was getting updates from their mum when she made her sporadic phone calls, always with an excuse about the signal being the reason she'd not rung earlier. Not that she knew much more about Harper than Jodie did, given their visits to her were only ever fleeting. And each time they'd managed to take their campervan to visit Harper, they'd not managed to come Jodie's way, blaming the congestion charges.

One thing Jodie had established over the years was that there was always a reason, and it was never their fault. They wouldn't recognise their own flaws if they were written on a list and placed on their windscreen. They were the kind of parents who had retired from the role once their children had turned eighteen and, as much as she understood their desire to travel, she'd had an expectation it might change in the current circumstances.

Jodie had invited them numerous times to come and see the

previous show. And because of Harper's accident they'd never made it to any of the subsequent performances of *Gingerbread*. So she'd extended the invite to the pantomime, asking them not to inform Harper about her current role. As their time was pretty much their own, she often thought it was such a shame they didn't make more of it. Of course, they thought they were by seeing more of the world, but she couldn't do the maths on how that was more important than spending time with their daughters. Especially given what they were both going through without each other.

None of that knowledge stemmed the optimism that eked out of Jodie at the start of every curtains up. For the first part of the show, it was only the main characters on the stage, and she remained in the wing with the five other members of the chorus on this side of the stage awaiting the first ensemble piece. It gave her a chance to scope out the audience, to see who was there. It was very likely that her parents would tell her if they were coming, but she still hoped that they'd surprise her. That their spontaneous natures would extend to not telling her and just turning up.

Every night that optimism had risen with the curtain, and then swiftly disappeared. It meant she always went on stage like a deflated balloon. It might not quite be the West End gig that she'd been aiming for, but she was performing on stage in London. Seven shows a week, and her parents hadn't yet managed to venture to one of them.

This particular show was going to be on for five weeks, running into January to allow for the school holidays. They had a matinee show on Christmas Eve and started again on Boxing Day, giving them only Christmas Day to celebrate.

Some of the cast did pantomime runs every year and therefore celebrated Christmas with their families in January. Some had their families coming to them so they didn't have to worry about spending half of those hours travelling. Some had booked to go to fancy restaurants or hotels and were clearly getting paid more than Jodie was. She was one of the few people with no plans and no idea what to do.

Their limited text conversations meant she couldn't discuss it with Harper, and she'd not bothered trying to have the conversation with her parents. Since they hadn't managed to visit at any other point, it seemed unlikely that they'd spare her the big day. She'd made the decision to stay put in London. Even if her lunch ended up being a turkey and stuffing sandwich, she'd at least enjoy an extra day off.

'You should join us!' Jasper, a fellow chorus member, offered when they were discussing everyone's plans.

'I wouldn't want to impose.'

'No, darling, you wouldn't be imposing. Half our flatmates are buggering off home. It'll only be me and Denna there.'

Denna was also in the chorus and had barely said a word to Jodie when they'd first started rehearsing. Jasper had always been nice to Jodie, but Denna seemed to disapprove of that. They lived in a flatshare along with some other dancers; they all knew each other after graduating from dance school in London. When she'd first met them, they'd seemed to define a clique, but as time had gone on and once the show had started, they'd both seemed to thaw slightly towards her. Which was a relief because they had to spend a lot of time together.

'Look, you don't have to give me an answer now, but if you end up without any other options then you should take up the offer. No one should be alone at Christmas.'

'I need to discuss it with my family. I've not had the chance to yet.' Or rather, she was avoiding it, knowing the plans might not be what she was hoping for.

As they continued to wait in the wings for their moment to arrive on stage, Jodie realised she'd never felt more alone in her life. Of course the circumstances meant that her parents needed to focus their attention on her sister. Of course they were going to be there for Harper as she learnt to adapt to her new situation. But Jodie had never thought she'd feel their absence so acutely. Or that in being separated from Harper, she'd end up separated from her parents as well. They'd always been flaky as if, having missed being hippies the first time round, they were making up for it now. But she'd thought some kind of parenting mode would have switched back on now that they both needed them. Apparently not. At least, not for her.

'Next time,' Denna said. 'Hopefully they'll be here next time.'

Jodie hadn't realised it had been so obvious that she was checking for them ahead of every performance.

Once more she went on stage with less gusto than she should. Her leaps weren't the highest she could do; her vocals weren't as loud as they should be. Because sometimes she wondered... what was the point?

When there was no one there to listen...

CHAPTER FOURTEEN

HARPER

Same old same.

The rehabilitation centre was strange at the weekends. Many of the healthcare professionals worked Monday to Friday, dealing only with the emergencies on a Saturday and Sunday. It left a strange lull about the place, as if even the atmosphere knew there were people missing. The change in routine was only emphasised by another of her parents' fly-by visits.

After telling her parents about her grand midweek adventure, a silence hung in the air. Whenever this happened, she always wondered how they filled their time together when they were away. And given that they'd been almost permanently away for over three years, it was a lot of time to fill. Perhaps that was the problem... they'd run out of things to say to each other. It made her sad that they'd also run out of things to say to her. Especially when their visits were always so fleeting every Saturday when they passed by.

When they'd first arrived a few days after her accident (they'd been holidaying in Spain and it had taken them two and a half days to return in the campervan), they'd waited until they knew there was nothing further they could do before heading off. That week they'd visited the New Forest.

The second trip had been Norfolk.

The third trip had been Kent.

This week's trip had been Dorset.

And the main focus of their discussion today was to tell her they planned to go to Wales, stopping in Oxfordshire on the way.

Over time, Harper had adjusted to having nomads as parents, but she'd thought that having one daughter in hospital and the other alone in London might have prompted them to stay nearby.

'Do you get day release at Christmas?' her mum asked.

'I don't think so. I'm an inpatient.' Harper glanced at her mum and wished she was able to read her mind. Because for years now, Harper had been the one to organise everything. Since her parents had sold their house, each Christmas Harper had been in charge of finding a pub that did lunch, the oven in the campervan not big enough to cater for more than two people. She'd not given the occasion much thought, given her current status. 'Why?'

'Oh, I was just wondering whether we should pop by that day?'

'Do you want to?'

'Of course, if you don't mind?'

'What about Jodie? What's she doing?' When Harper had been gearing up for her rehab here, she'd not even thought about the fact that the timeframe spanned over Christmas and New Year. Even though it had initially been her idea, it seemed wrong not to see her sister for their family tradition. Even if that tradition was now a pub meal.

'She's going to be busy with the show. She only has that day off.'

'What? So I won't see her?' Harper felt the disappointment wind its way around her. She'd thought they'd have a reprieve of their agreement for that one day.

'I think she's happy doing her own thing, just this once...'

'Really?' It wasn't that she didn't believe her mum, but she would have preferred to clarify these things directly with her sister, rather than via their whimsical parents.

'We can make up for it once you've been discharged.'

It bothered Harper that she wouldn't get to see her sister, but she knew it wouldn't be logistically possible. The train would be about a two-hour journey, so possible on a normal day, but as they didn't tend to run over Christmas and Boxing Day, it would prevent any travel. Ideally, her parents would pick her up, but as they hadn't ever invited either of them into the camper, neither of them were about to ask. Some things had to be volunteered.

'When you speak to her, can you tell her that I'll miss her and that I love her?'

'I'm sure if you asked her she'd come and visit. It seems so silly that the pair of you aren't in touch like usual. It's strange for us, so it must feel really odd to you.'

'I know it's odd and at times it's hard to explain. Let's just say I lost part of myself in that accident. And having my identical sister as a mirror, who is no longer my exact image, has been tough. I need to find myself again, and a new kind of strength, on my own. It was really hard at first, but it's getting easier. I want to feel more confident. I want to be the one able to go to her rather than her having to come to me.'

'Jodie would accept you at whatever stage you're at. You know that.'

'Yes, but I don't want her halting her own progress to watch. Especially when I'm the only one that can do this for me.'

'If you're sure?'

Harper nodded. Because sometimes a nod in the right place was better than saying what was really on her mind.

By the time her parents had gone, she was more tired than after a full day of training. She loved them, but they were very intense. Normally she had her sister to spread the load, but at the moment their magnifying glass was concentrated very much in one direction. As a twin, she'd always hoped to be the centre of attention, but these certainly weren't the circumstances in which she'd wanted to obtain that status. Now the spotlight was on her, she wondered how to get rid of it.

To break up the monotony after her parents had left, Harper decided to explore all the corridors in the rehab centre that she'd never been along. Many places, like the therapy services, were locked up over the weekend so there wasn't much of interest to see, but having gone round the lake in the week, she'd realised she was capable of longer distances than she'd been attempting. She was even pretty fast, she realised, having beaten Maceo. Admittedly, she'd had a head start, but the gap had widened rather than reduced.

There was a lingering sense of something unfinished when she got to the entrance. Like a half-formed thought that she couldn't catch hold of. It brought Jodie to the forefront of her mind, but rather than dwelling on how much she was missing her, she tried to concentrate on what their reunion would be like, how it would feel when she could navigate London and get to the theatre by herself.

Whatever the thought had been, it didn't fully form before she caught it. For the next couple of hours, having found a corridor where there was no traffic and only the odd person floating about, she timed herself racing from one end to the other. Each time she tried to push herself that much more until her muscles burned and she knew she'd reached the stage where she wouldn't improve any further. She was surprised to learn how fast she was. And once she'd rested her arms for an hour or so, they recovered easily, and she almost felt she could do it again.

Yes, in three more weeks she would be champing at the bit to see her sister. Because by then she'd be unstoppable. Not worried about comparisons because she'd have her own set of qualities for people to admire. She wouldn't be in anyone's shadow because she would have done enough to shine.

She just wasn't sure who she was trying to achieve that for. Was it for Harper, or for Jodie?

CHAPTER FIFTEEN

JODIE

'Tis the season!

At the time, it had seemed like the world's greatest idea. She might have a hectic schedule, but when Vince had called her to say there was a last-minute closure for a few hours at the café while their equipment underwent a yearly service, she saw it as a sign. The heavens opening up an opportunity.

Because she knew it was a rare chance, she had to act on it quickly. Not that the journey there had been particularly quick. She spent the whole time worrying about getting back for her evening performance, but it would be worth it for five minutes with her sister. Ever since she'd had the pang she'd been wanting to act on it, so she figured for once she'd be spontaneous.

The first blow came when she saw her parents' bright orange campervan in the car park. It was so distinctive there was no mistaking it for any other. She'd known they were visiting occasionally, but if she'd planned this visit, she would have ensured they weren't there at the same time. It's not that she didn't want to be reunited with her parents, but her sister was first on her list without a doubt.

The second blow came as she made her way to the ward and overheard their conversation before they knew she was there.

'...And having my identical sister as a mirror, who is no longer my exact image, has been tough. I need to find myself again, and a new kind of strength, on my own. It was really hard at first, but it's getting easier. I want to feel more confident. I want to be the one able to go to her rather than her having to come to me...'

Hearing those words brought everything home for Jodie. She was desperate to go over and give her sister a hug, but she suddenly realised she was there for entirely selfish reasons. *She* wanted to see her sister. *She* wanted to talk to her. It wasn't the other way round. And by being there she wasn't giving her sister the chance to flourish like she needed to. She needed to wait until Harper was ready.

Rather than declare herself like she'd planned to, she slipped away, unnoticed by her family. Hearing her sister's reasons reiterated why sticking to the plan was important. Being here was selfish, but knowing that leaving was the right thing to do didn't stop her tears on the long journey home.

She missed her sister more than ever in the following days, but she was more determined to last the six weeks for Harper's benefit. As far back as she could remember, Harper had been the organised one and it was about time Jodie worked out a plan for her life so that when they were reunited, Harper would be proud of her. Not that she had much of a plan currently. She had three more shifts at the café and three more performances before Christmas Day. She wasn't sure why she was counting down. It wasn't like she was getting a nice break as a result. Other than one extra day off.

Antoine and his flatmates were taking a trip to Brighton

beach. They didn't celebrate Christmas, but liked to mark it in a different way. It had become an annual pilgrimage because no one else was ever there. They'd once made the mistake of going on Boxing Day but it hadn't had the same quality with so many people out on post-Christmas walks. He'd invited Jodie along and, even though it would have meant being pinned into the middle seat in the back, it had been a tempting offer. Until she learnt they were leaving before dawn on Christmas Day to avoid the Christmas Eve traffic. They planned to snooze in the car or on the beach for a bit once they arrived.

Jodie would only just be finished with the show when they were about to head off, so however tempting it had been, Christmas wouldn't be a particularly restful day with no sleep beforehand. She might not be spending it with her family as usual, but there was still an opportunity to eat turkey until she was stuffed and fall asleep on the sofa listening to the Queen's speech. Traditions were traditions, after all. So she took Jasper and Denna up on their offer. She couldn't look a gift horse in the mouth, so she checked it was still okay ahead of their next performance.

'They've headed back home already, you know,' Jasper said with an air of disapproval towards his flatmates. 'Honestly, they don't know they're born with some of the easy hours they get. Okay for some, isn't it?'

Jodie nodded agreement, though she wasn't entirely sure what she was agreeing with. It was hard to add any comment when they weren't people she'd ever met.

'You should come over sooner. Are you still staying in that crumby pub?'

Jodie nodded again. She quite liked that some conversations with Jasper didn't require any of her verbal input.

'Well, gosh. You can't be there over Christmas. You can stay in the boys' room. They aren't due back until January and the rent's all paid up, so save yourself a few bob. You can just help out with the groceries.'

'Really?' Jodie did have to speak at this. To have a cheap place to stay for a while, especially over Christmas when everything seemed to have added expense, felt like a dream. An unexpected one that she'd be foolish to turn down. Especially when she was missing Harper so much.

'Of course. Just make sure you keep the room tidy. Pack your stuff tonight and bring it to the theatre tomorrow. Then you can come home with me!' Jasper said the last part with such glee that it would have made anyone smile.

By the time Jodie had packed her things and was heading to work again the next day, there was an ominous feeling in the pit of her stomach. The room she'd been staying in wasn't perfect, but it had become home for the past few weeks. The landlord had been good about when she made her payments and had kept the bookings clear for her. In a way, she felt like she was doing him a disservice by just upping and leaving. But she couldn't turn down rent-free accommodation for a week, possibly more. That would save her enough money for the Christmas presents she hadn't managed to purchase yet.

By the time she'd got through another shift at the café, Vince's moans not abating for the festive period, followed by another pantomime performance, she was ready to fall into bed. But as she wasn't returning to her own space, that wasn't going to happen. Saving money wasn't going to come without its cost.

'We need to host a little welcome party for our Jo,' Jasper said, swinging open a drinks cabinet that was as well-stocked as the pub in the village where Jodie had grown up. 'What can I get you? We'll have a little drinky-poos to celebrate and then I'll show you your room.'

Jodie ignored the fact he'd abbreviated her name. Even though she'd been living above a pub, she wasn't in the habit of having a regular nightcap. She wasn't going to fight against the tide, though, when Jasper was only being welcoming. It was a far more generous spirit than she'd found anywhere else she'd stayed.

'I'll have a G and T if you've got it?'

'But of course! And how very Barbara Windsor of you. I'm sure it was her favourite drink, considering the number of times she ordered it on *EastEnders*.'

Jodie smiled. She drank so infrequently that she didn't recognise half the bottles in the cabinet. And she'd never watched the popular soap to know.

'Take a seat, lovely. I'll sort this and bring it over.'

'You want the usual, Denna?' Jasper called.

'Of course, darling,' she drawled as she came out of the toilet. 'Let's get this party started.'

Jodie wondered if it was Christmas already and she just had her days mixed up.

'Well, I can tell you have, darling.' Jasper gently pinched Denna's nose before twirling her around as if it were a dance move.

Once they'd stopped fooling around, they stared so intimately at each other for a moment that Jodie felt like a gooseberry. She hadn't thought they were a couple, but that didn't mean they couldn't enjoy each other's company. She'd noticed there tended to be casual relationships occurring in the background of most productions she'd been involved in. At college she'd put it down to all the teenage hormones bouncing about, but perhaps that concept wasn't going to exit the building for a few years yet. Or certainly not this flat.

'I'll fix you a double to get things started.'

Started? Alcohol at this time of night when she needed to work two jobs tomorrow might end Jodie.

'I'll just have the one tonight. I'll have to get up earlier than both of you.'

'Oh gosh. Why don't you give it up? That boss of yours sounds like a monster.'

'I don't want to leave him in the lurch before Christmas...'

In truth, it wasn't Vince, but Antoine that she would worry about. He's the one she'd miss if she left. In the time she'd been there, another two of the early morning serving staff had left. Staff retention was so poor that Antoine had already joked about the fact that she'd need a long-service award before long.

'Burning the candle at both ends then, sweetie? We can always give you a little something to help with that.'

Jodie knew exactly what Jasper meant, and she knew what Denna had been doing in the bathroom on her return. There was plenty of it about, but she hadn't done it and she never planned to. She preferred to let her body live by its natural biorhythms. 'Nah, I'm gonna go with sleep as the answer to my problems.'

'Knock this down your neck and you'll get some proper sleep.' Jasper passed her the definitely home-measured G & T.

She took a sip – it was so potent it took her breath away. 'You're not joking!'

'Denna and I like to work hard and play hard. It's the secret to a long life.'

'Do your flatmates live by the same philosophy?' Jodie had realised the space was full with just the three of them. She couldn't imagine it with two other people trying to live in the cramped space.

'Not so much on the working hard front. Hence why they get to enjoy more than a week off over Christmas. But never mind them. Let's concentrate on us.'

'Shall we stick the karaoke on?' Denna asked.

'When haven't we stuck the karaoke on?' Jasper laughed, moving his concentration away from Jodie.

It was a relief. She'd felt like he was about to scrutinise her, and she didn't know how much they knew. Whether they realised she was the sister of the dancer whose life had so dramatically changed. They struck her as the kind of people who'd love getting all the gossip, but she wasn't going to trade that for her free room. She wished she had spoken to Harper, to fill her in on the past few weeks. But then Jodie remembered Harper telling her parents she wanted to be strong enough to make her way to Jodie, not the other way round.

'Kylie? That's rhetorical, of course. I'll stick her on first. Are you going to join in?' Denna asked Jodie.

'Do you mind if I go and pop my things in my room? I'm going to change out of my dancing gear and then I'll join you.'

'Let me give you the tour,' Jasper offered.

Jodie really wanted to go straight to her room and get to bed, but she couldn't be rude in the face of their kindness.

'Here's our little kitchenette. Tiny, but obviously none of us really have time to cook, so that's not a problem.'

'Great,' Jodie commented, uncertain what she should be saying.

'There's a shared shower room. Again, no time for baths so it does the job. The toilet's separate, thank goodness, given how long some of these divas take doing their hair.'

Denna glanced over to the tour that had barely seen them needing to leave the front room and did a spectacular eyeroll. 'Says *the* diva himself.'

'Ignore her,' he said. 'Let me show you where you'll be staying.'

At last. Fortunately, the flat wasn't big enough for the tour to take up any length of time. All the doors led off the boxy lounge area and there was only one remaining, which made her wonder what the usual arrangements were. Jasper led her into a room with a bunk bed. There were no windows, only another door.

'Denna and I are in this room. It's a bit of a strange set-up, but that's one of the reasons it's cheaper than a lot of properties round here. And I'm a big fan of cheap when it gives us more opportunity to party.' Jasper necked some of the lurid blue drink he was holding in what must have been a bid to demonstrate the party spirit.

Jodie might have been inclined to follow suit, but it turned out she was a fan of her windpipe and didn't want to risk burning it on concentrated alcohol.

'Oh, great,' Jodie said, even though it wasn't great at all. It was okay at most. 'So, where will I sleep?'

'Through here.' Jasper opened what looked like a cupboard door to reveal a further bedroom with a bunk bed and a similar format to the first room, only this one had a window. Someone had obviously divided one large bedroom into two smaller ones so they could charge more rent.

'What if I need the loo in the night?' It wasn't unknown for her to have her granny-bladder moments in the early hours of the morning.

'The boys sometimes do it in a bottle and chuck it out the next day. But if peeing in a bottle isn't your thing, you'll just have to make your way through quietly.'

If the alcohol content wasn't enough to put her off her drink, the thought of having to disturb anyone's sleep might be enough to.

'I'll try and cross my legs.'

'Oh, don't be doing that on my account. That's the last thing we want.' Jasper said it in such a way that she wondered if he was flirting.

'I'll sort my things for a bit, if that's all right?'

'You go ahead. Take your pick of the beds, but stick with, it if that's okay? I only want to change one lot of bedding. Don't be long,' Jasper said, before closing the door.

Jodie collapsed onto the bottom bunk. She wasn't even going to attempt to use the top one. She inspected the room a bit closer. It was tidy with very little in it other than the bunk bed and a side table. It reminded her of the hostel and she wondered if she'd need to put up a makeshift curtain in order to protect her privacy. Although, she reminded herself, she had this space to herself for now. Privacy probably wasn't the thing she needed to worry about. The bigger worry was if Jasper and Denna decided to block the door as a joke. It was an odd way to regard the pair, given they'd been kind enough to offer her a place to stay for a while. But something about them was giving her bad-energy vibes. Ones that she wasn't able to explain. Ones that she'd normally share and dissect with her sister, but she knew she'd have to hold on to those updates for now.

When she re-joined them, they were eager for her to join in with the singing and carry on drinking. She humoured them for another half hour or so, but knowing she had to get up to do another shift at the café meant she needed her bed. As always, it had been a long day.

'Don't be a killjoy! Stay up! We're having so much fun!' Jasper pleaded.

Jodie wondered whether their neighbours thought it was fun if this was how they amused themselves every evening. Although, they were above a takeaway shop that was now closed, so perhaps there weren't any neighbours to annoy.

'Honestly, I need to get to bed so I can be ready for work tomorrow. I'll try not to wake you in the morning,' she said, realising they may well still be in bed around the time she would be leaving.

The bad energy she'd sensed earlier became more tangible as the night went on. Because they didn't stop their singing at a reasonable hour. It went on until four in the morning and their journey to bed wasn't a quiet one. Jodie lost count of the number of times she'd just drifted off only to be woken by more noise. She'd had better sleep when she'd been sharing with a potentially murderous roommate. Even the hubbub of the pub had always abated at a sensible hour.

In the morning, when she made her way through their room, she was of a mind to not worry about whatever noise she made. A fair level of revenge, she thought, given that it would only be imitating what they'd done to her.

But this was a free stay, she reminded herself. For a short while, she was at their mercy, and as she didn't want to rock that boat, she tiptoed her way through and hoped there wouldn't be a repeat performance every night.

CHAPTER SIXTEEN

HARPER

Happy Christmas, sis!

Everything about the festive season had been different this year. There had been an adjustment after their parents had sold the family home and they'd switched to pub meals, but not seeing her sister was a huge shift. So much so that she was trying to ignore the fact it was Christmas. For the first time in her life she was going for the bah humbug approach to the day.

None of them could have imagined at the start of the year exactly how different this festive period would end up looking. Harper and Jodie, separated from each other for the first time. Jodie remaining in London because of her show commitments and spending the day with her friends, and Harper having turkey dinner from the catering team at the Neurological Rehabilitation Centre, with their parents doing a quick stop-by in the campervan to see her. It didn't seem fair that they weren't going to see Jodie as well, but Harper had realised some time ago that her parents never liked to be told what to do. The only way to get them to do anything was to make them think it was their own idea. These days it felt like even though she and Jodie were the children, they had to act like the parents, and she didn't have the energy to guide their decisions this year.

In their three-word messages over the past few days, she and Jodie had managed to establish that they would celebrate Christmas properly once they were reunited. But Harper still wished her sister happy Christmas in her morning message and thought about her for most of the day. She wanted to know what she was doing. Whether her day involved turkey. Whether she had any gifts to open, given that her parents had also agreed to wait to exchange gifts until they were all together. She wanted to know if she was happy or sad, in good company or alone. There was so much the messages didn't convey for a day like today. A day that should be about family. It was hard not to feel guilty that she was the only one who would be seeing their parents. That hadn't been her choice, but it didn't ease how she was feeling about it.

Her parents' visit came with the usual awkwardness of not knowing what to talk about. It was like they'd exhausted all subjects and now there was that weighted question of when she'd ever be better. But, of course, she would never be the Harper who had left to live in London. That Harper was never returning to them and sometimes she wondered if their visits were as much about learning to accept that as they were to provide her with support.

This Harper was who she was now. She was coming to realise that even though the number of limbs that did as they were told had changed, essentially she hadn't. She was still as determined and focussed as ever. And for now she was putting that energy into the rehabilitation she was receiving while she was here. Today, that was on hold, though. The usual therapy staff enjoying an extra couple of bank holidays off work.

When it came to saying goodbye to her parents, she wheeled all the way to the car park to see them off. It was oddly early, but without presents to open they'd decided to go and watch the Queen's speech as they'd booked themselves into a hotel room for a change ahead of their Christmas dinner. Their first Christmas meal without their girls since they'd become parents, Francesca and Tony had said about a hundred times that morning. It wasn't helping Harper's quest to forget what day it actually was.

'Are you sure you're going to be okay?' her mum asked as she hovered by the campervan, hugging her coat around her against the cold.

'Look, we've already said this isn't our Christmas. I'm going to treat it like a normal bank holiday. I suggest you do the same. Just make sure you call Jodie and give her my love. Tell her I can't wait to see her soon.'

It hurt that they weren't going to see her sister. A dam of tears was threatening to spill over, but Harper was determined to hold on to them. She didn't want to cry in front of her parents.

'I will. And happy Christmas, love. I know we said we wouldn't do presents, but I couldn't help but get a little something for you and your sister.' Her mum passed her a neatly wrapped box in such a way that any onlookers might think they were trading illicit substances.

'You shouldn't have, Mum.'

'Shush! Don't let on to your dad. I snuck this one in, but I'll be doing a proper Christmas shop as usual, only it'll be in the January sales so I might get more for our money.'

'Sorry I don't have anything for you today. There aren't many shops round here.'

'Don't you worry at all! This is just me stretching the rules a little. It's my privilege as your mum.'

Francesca took her into a hug and she made her dad come and join them, even though he wasn't too keen on public displays of affection. It was Christmas, after all, and they were in a car park with barely anyone about.

But Harper didn't *feel* the hugs, not when it was an incomplete circle. Not when a family hug shouldn't exist without her sister. She had to remind herself that she would be there when they *actually* celebrated Christmas. That today was not that day in its usual context.

After that, Harper headed back to the ward and did her best not to think about what day it was and that she and her twin sister were alone. At least she'd seen her parents. So she didn't get to feel sorry for herself.

But that didn't stop that empty feeling from nestling in her stomach.

Even though she was busy trying to pretend it wasn't Christmas Day, Harper was glad to have a present to mark it all the same. It gave her something to look forward to.

She put off opening it as long as possible, taking advantage of the peace and quiet to explore more of the hospital. She cruised along corridors she'd never come across before and investigated avenues that she perhaps shouldn't have. Still, if no one was here to tell her she shouldn't be in certain places, did it matter?

All her exploring didn't alleviate her sadness. She longed to pick up the phone and speak to Jodie. To know how she was. To know that she was getting stronger as well. But it was only another two and a bit weeks before her rehabilitation would be complete, and she shook herself as a reminder to not be sentimental because it was Christmas.

Dinner was served in the day room with the other patients, rather than at their bedsides as usual. Harper joined in the fun, and even though she didn't know anyone there especially well, apart from in passing, exchanging crackers and corny jokes with virtual strangers didn't turn out to be all that bad. The same couldn't be said for the dried-out turkey and stuffing that the somewhat lumpy gravy couldn't entirely cure. It wasn't a patch on the dinners she usually had, but it was edible enough and she was thankful to be sitting here eating a Christmas dinner, realising her story might have been completely different. This didn't seem like a bad deal by any standards.

Once dinner was over, she decided to get an early night. Before she did, she took a moment to open her present. Her mum always went all-out on the wrapping, and this year she'd gone for tartan wrapping paper and matching ribbon with sprigs of holly. It always looked like it had taken ages and it seemed a shame to spoil it, but the urge to open any presents always over-ruled that feeling.

Once the ribbon was off, the wrapping peeled off easily. Inside was a navy blue box with gold edging. It was from a local independent jeweller near to where they used to live on the Welsh border.

Opening the box and pulling back the tissue paper, Harper discovered a gold necklace with two small gold discs attached. When she took a closer look, she could see one disc had an H and the other a J. Harper and Jodie. Jodie and Harper. Always together. Until now.

It was a sweet, sentimental gift that made Harper happy as much as it made her sad. Inside, there was also a note from her mum.

Dear Harper,

I thought this necklace was beautiful, like my two beautiful girls. You might be apart for a while, but you're always connected.

Love, Mum xx

Harper placed the necklace around her neck and wondered

if Jodie had an identical one. Whether her mother had made sure to send it ready for them to be united while apart. The thought made her consider the strange set of rules she'd put them under. Perhaps six weeks was too long? Perhaps it was time to give this gig up? She was much stronger than she had been. It was weeks on from the point when she was wobbly even when sitting. She could do so much more now...

But then she remembered why it had been necessary. In her whole life she'd never been able to concentrate solely on herself, and right now that was how it had to be. Because right now she didn't have the confidence to go any further than the hospital car park by herself. She'd managed it with Maceo and Aden, but she wasn't ready to venture outside the hospital grounds alone. When she was, she'd be heading straight for her sister.

Deciding, as it was Christmas, it was the time to ignore the rules, she plunged in for a second three-word message of the day. Taking a selfie with her necklace in view, she sent the photo through to Jodie along with the message *Are we matching?*

She'd thought she would get a simple message of confirmation, but when she didn't get a response, she didn't know what to think. Perhaps it had been a thoughtless message – she didn't know if Jodie had received her necklace yet.

Ever since the accident, even though she wasn't with her sister, there hadn't been many moments when she'd felt alone. She'd been too busy for that, with far too many healthcare professionals requiring her time. But loneliness was her only companion right now. And the original determinedness to maintain a distance from her sister had lost its intensity. Surely seeing her sister wouldn't do any harm to anything other than her ego? But there was a threshold and her own confidence standing in the way.

When she went to bed, she held the necklace in her palm, falling asleep with the chain laced between her fingers. She dreamt of her and Jodie and the unbreakable bond that existed between them, her phone in her other hand in the hope she'd hear from her soon.

Because as bonds went, right now theirs felt pretty broken. Perhaps it was time to work out how to fix it.

CHAPTER SEVENTEEN

JODIE

Happy non-Christmas, sis!

Nothing about the last few days had been Jodie's usual Christmas fare. Christmas Eve wasn't usually a raucous affair of alcohol and karaoke, for starters. Having refused every evening to join in for more than half an hour, using work as an excuse, she'd realised she couldn't be a killjoy for another night.

She'd also come to the realisation that she wanted to join in. She wanted to have fun for a change. Everything had felt so serious since Harper's accident, and she hadn't really let her hair down. She almost felt that if she didn't act responsibly, she would somehow be doing her sister a disservice. Or that something else might go wrong.

However, it was Christmas. Even if she wasn't celebrating like usual, it didn't mean she wasn't allowed to enjoy the day. If she couldn't let her hair down for one night in these unusual circumstances, then she didn't know when she could.

So she did. She stayed up way past her usual bedtime. She sang many questionable songs and drank alcoholic beverages of varying colours. She might have been in danger of needing her stomach pumped if Mother Nature hadn't worked that out for her using more natural remedies. Come Christmas Day, Jodie was hanging so badly she might as well have given it all up and started a life as a tree decoration. Remaining static seemed to be the only thing she should – or could – do today.

When she stirred enough to be able to work out where she was, she kicked a bucket in her attempts to get out of bed. She held her head, the movement alone enough to bring the nausea back. Never before had she felt the need to pray that she'd get to the bathroom quickly enough. Denna and Jasper weren't in their room when she passed through, which surprised her. They'd been going at it harder than she had, although it turned out practice was required for these occasions.

'Merry Christmas!' they both chorused when Jodie made it to the lounge area.

She couldn't even reciprocate the good wishes before bolting to the loo. If her churning stomach wasn't bad enough, no amount of leg-crossing would stem the flow. She made it in time, but she didn't get a chance to breathe a sigh of relief as Jasper was outside.

'Oh, lovely! You feeling it a bit?'

'Ugh,' Jodie replied.

'Coffee? We've got the turkey in the oven already. Only two hours and it'll be time for Christmas dinner.'

Considering Jodie was in the lavatory and deciding whether she'd be able to reach the bathroom sink in time if her nausea tipped over, she really didn't want to be having a conversation through the bathroom door about food. Especially as she'd not been clever enough to lock it and, if he chose to, Jasper could walk in at any minute.

'Coffee might help,' she managed to say.

Really, she wasn't too sure if her stomach was up to coffee. And it was far too early for any thoughts about solid food. She needed several hours of recovery before she would be able to contemplate a slice of toast, let alone a roast dinner.

She spent around quarter of an hour completing relatively simple tasks, but she wasn't sure it had left her feeling any more human. It might be Christmas Day, but she just wanted to crawl back to bed. As soon as she was out of the safety of the bathroom, her temporary flatmates had other ideas.

'Time for presents!' Jasper chorused.

Jodie was left wondering how one person could chorus, but then reasoned it was probably something to do with the ringing in her head. That and his occupation giving him the capabilities.

'I'll go and get mine!' Denna said.

'Me too,' Jodie said, hoping no one would mind if she took a lie-down before coming back.

She was glad she'd had the foresight to get them both a small gift. After all, as they were hosting her on Christmas Day it seemed polite. After hearing Jasper's excited shrieks, she gave up on any ideas of lying down; she'd have to save that for later.

'A pint of water for our dancing queen. I thought you might need that before anything stronger.'

Jodie took the drink gratefully and swooped on it as if it were a life force. She'd never needed fluid more in her life.

'Did I really sing "Dancing Queen"?'

'Several times. A favourite, apparently?'

'Oh God.' 'Dancing Queen' wasn't her favourite song, it was Harper's. Had she confessed to that fact last night? How much more had she told them? She didn't recall having any emotional outbursts, but she also didn't recall singing the same song repeatedly.

'It was nice to see you with your hair down. More of the same today, please!' Denna flopped onto the sofa next to Jasper and invited Jodie to join them.

She did, but with cautious movements, wedging herself to

one side of Jasper. Currently the flat was moving as if she were on a boat, rather than on solid ground.

'Me first!' Jasper said, like an excitable child. 'One for you and one for you.' He passed Denna a parcel that appeared to be some kind of inflatable covered in wrapping paper, and he gave Jodie a small gift bag.

'Me next,' Denna said, passing them both identically sized parcels.

'And me next,' Jodie said, passing them both small wrapped gifts.

'Go!' Jasper said, as he started attacking the wrapping paper as if leaving it in place was creating an emergency situation.

'I love it!' Denna cheered before anyone else had managed to open a parcel. Not even Jasper with his vicious attack method. Denna was now the proud owner of an inflatable flamingo.

'I know how much you love flamingos and I couldn't resist,' Jasper said, temporarily pausing his efforts.

Jodie opened the small gift box from Denna first. Keeping with the theme, she was now the proud owner of some flamingo earrings. 'Thank you, they're lovely!'

'I wasn't too sure what your tastes are, so I decided to get something that should be universally liked, and I'm afraid if you don't like flamingos, we can't be friends.'

The statement made Jodie smile. It was one way to work out if friendships were compatible.

'Oh my God, I love it!' Jasper squeaked from the other end of the sofa. He had a matching necklace to Jodie's earrings that he was holding against his chest. 'Do it up for me, lovely?'

They spent a couple of minutes making sure Jasper's necklace was secured and Jodie's earrings were in before moving on to their next gifts.

Jasper and Denna were quicker than she was and both squealed their delight at her gifts. They were a token London gift she'd seen at a craft fair she'd chanced upon. In the boxes were two flat pebbles with Big Ben painted on them. As none of them were originally from the big city, she thought it was a nice memento to keep for a time when that might not be the case.

'You didn't make these, did you?' Jasper asked.

Jodie explained where she'd discovered them, and that she didn't have a hidden talent.

'Your turn!' Jasper said, now that there was only one present left to open.

Jodie undid the ribbon on the small gift bag and wondered if it was another piece of jewellery. Inside was a smaller bag, which contained a small green lump.

'What is it?' Jodie asked, not having a clue.

'Have a sniff – that should tell you.'

Jodie wasn't too sure about sniffing items that she couldn't easily identify by sight. But without meaning to she caught a waft of a distinctive aroma and knew instantly what it was.

'I thought you might like some to have a chill at some point!' Jasper suggested.

'Also, he needed a gift that was on hand,' Denna said.

'Shut up, friend,' Jasper replied. 'You can have some for pudding. It might help with that hangover.'

'Thanks,' Jodie replied, not sure if she should be thankful when she'd been given drugs unsolicited. Although, as she'd accepted the present, was that still true?

The other thing she didn't do was give it back. Because even though it was something she'd never tried, right now she was tempted. If for a short while it eased her worries, then it would be a welcome experience.

'Right, I'm going to finish preparing dinner while you delicate flowers get some rest. You both look like you definitely need more sleep. Here, pass me the flamingo and it can keep me company.'

Their new inflatable friend was passed over like a mascot before both girls returned to their rooms.

Getting back into bed provided an unparalleled level of relief. Jodie's head was starting to pound and the nausea was only just beginning to settle. Surprisingly, the water and coffee combo had helped.

It was some hours later that they were all dining off lap trays around the small coffee table, eating more than anyone would have thought possible of all three of them. Jasper had done an excellent job, not far off her mother's efforts in the days she'd owned a big enough kitchen.

'Ready for pudding?' Jasper asked with a suggestive raise of his eyebrow after they'd finished and cleared away the plates.

Jodie had been about to confirm that she wouldn't be partaking when her phone rang.

Saved by the bell. Literally.

She mouthed that it was her mum and made her way into her boxed-in bedroom to chat in private.

'Happy Christmas, Mum,' she said.

'Is it, though?' It was unusual for her mum to be despondent.

'But you've seen Harper today? And she's okay?'

'Yes, love. But it's not the same, is it? Not having us all together. We'd be stuffed by now and in need of a nap. I have to apologise, I gave your sister an extra present, but I didn't know where to send yours to, so I've still got it for now.'

'But you haven't asked where I'm staying. How would you know if you haven't asked?'

It was almost like her mum wanted Jodie to feel sorry for her. And she did. She felt sorry for all of them. But it wasn't just her mum in this situation, and the fact she'd not seen her parents since Harper had been in hospital in London meant she wasn't the only one feeling hard done by. It was hard to summon any sympathy for her parents when they hadn't given up their lifestyle. Not when she was feeling this sorry for herself.

'You've been moving about, dear. If you don't have a permanent address, where would I send it?'

Jodie decided not to point out that as her parents were in the same situation and had found ways around it, then they could have worked it out. It could have been sent to the theatre, or the café. Or – but this was really wishful thinking – she could have delivered it herself. Instead, she listened to her mother's humdrum complaints, while wanting to shout that she didn't care. Not when she was the daughter who had been abandoned.

As she listened, Jodie was beginning to realise that her mother *blamed* her. She was the daughter who should have gone second. She was the daughter who'd made it across the road undamaged and was able to continue her life as planned. She was the daughter she'd not been able to look in the eye since it had happened. No wonder her mother hadn't come to the show. She loved her sister with a passion, but it *wasn't* her fault that this had happened. It was a quiet side street. Every dancer there had been doing the same thing without thinking there was any imminent danger...

Rather than confront her over the phone, Jodie opted to make all the right noises in all the right places. She didn't want to argue on Christmas Day. She could save that for their fake Christmas Day. Wasn't that what family gatherings were for?

Once she was off the phone, she was left with a deep sense of loneliness. She'd known when they'd moved to London that this year would be different. But it wasn't even close to what she'd imagined. It wasn't just that she wasn't with her family. She felt like she'd been left to float adrift. She'd become unanchored, and while her sister was being supported by her parents, they didn't have any time for her. She realised why as she thought about how easy it would have been for them to get her gift to her: the girls should have been looking after each other and, in their eyes, Jodie had failed Harper.

So when she re-joined her colleagues in the front room (she'd not worked out if they were friends or foes yet), she indulged in the pudding. *All* the puddings. She didn't say no to any of the things that were offered, because it turned out that while she might have her spine intact, that didn't mean *she* was.

CHAPTER EIGHTEEN

HARPER

How are you?

'Are you ready?' Maceo asked.

Having not had a reply to her second – strictly speaking, not allowed – message to her sister, Harper had been glued to her phone. She'd sent a further message ridiculously early and was still waiting to hear. It took all her strength to look away from the screen. All she wanted to do was call Jodie, and she felt silly for not having done so already.

'Ready for what?' Harper asked.

'Your Christmas present. I know it's a day late, but my mum wouldn't let me leave the house yesterday.'

'Right.'

'Are you okay?'

Harper didn't think she was. 'I haven't heard back from my sister...'

'What? You didn't speak to her yesterday?'

'We exchanged our usual three-word message, but I sent an extra one, what with it being Christmas and everything. I thought she'd reply. But she hasn't, and she's not replied to today's message yet.'

'Did you try calling her?'

'No. I know it's stupid, but I want us to stick to the agreement. Except I haven't. I've sent an extra message, and I thought she'd do the same.'

'It's early yet. Try not to fret, she might still be in bed. Let's go and enjoy your Christmas present and if you haven't had your three-word message by the time we're back, then you're allowed to worry and we'll plan something.'

'We're going out?'

'Bring a coat and follow me.'

'Where are we going?' Harper had been expecting another quiet day in hospital with it being a bank holiday.

'That would spoil the surprise.'

Harper wasn't sure she liked surprises. Getting hit by a London cab had been her last surprise and look where that had got her. She'd quite like to leave surprises on the shelf and stick with the things she loved.

She followed Maceo out of the rehabilitation centre and stopped beside him as he demonstrated some jazz hands in front of the limo that was waiting for them.

'Ta-da!'

'Is this for us?' Harper asked.

'But of course. Care to take a seat?'

The chauffeur had obviously been briefed on how he would have to help and was ready to take Harper's chair.

'Where are we going?'

'Wherever you like.'

'What do you mean?'

'Exactly that. Well, almost. The limit is a twenty-mile radius. I figured you might enjoy a slice of freedom for a while.'

'Anywhere?' The only place Harper wanted to go was to see

her sister, but that was over twenty miles away. Perhaps they would agree if she offered to pay for the extra petrol?

'I don't go inside the M25, though,' the chauffeur said, as if he were reading her mind.

That left Harper not knowing where to request. Her only desire right now was to be with Jodie. 'Any recommendations?' she asked instead.

'What do you feel like doing?' Maceo asked. 'The country-side? Shopping? Golf? The choice is yours.'

Harper didn't want to point out that the choice wasn't really hers if she was limited by the number of miles they travelled and London wasn't an option. But she wasn't going to be mean-spirited when this was a thoughtful gift from Maceo. Some might even say it was romantic, but she was going to ignore that vibe. Although given how smartly he'd dressed, maybe she shouldn't.

'Shopping,' she said, hoping it was the least romantic option.

'How about the shopping village? That's less than an hour away and, given it's Boxing Day, the sales should be good.'

Harper nodded, even though she realised it would be busy and she didn't know if she was okay with busy yet. She hadn't experienced it since becoming a wheelchair user. But if she was going to get back to real life at some point, she had to deal with these hurdles.

Before she'd thought about it in too much depth, they were on their way. Maceo had joined her in the back seat, and rather than chatting they were both staring out of their respective windows, the chauffeur having promised to take them the most scenic route. As they travelled along the country lanes, she wondered if this was the kind of thing he did for weddings.

She'd become so used to Maceo's upbeat personality that his quiet demeanour was unnerving.

'Are you okay?' Harper ventured to ask.

'Yeah.'

'Why so quiet? What's on your mind?' She wasn't going to take his first answer today, sensing it wasn't entirely true. She'd seen an advert advising that it was worth asking twice when someone appeared to be struggling.

'It's silly stuff.'

'It's not silly if it's bothering you.'

Maceo took a big sigh and looked at her properly for the first time. 'You know sometimes you have these expectations within yourself about how things will be, and when the reality doesn't match up to that it can be hard to accept?'

'I think I know what you mean, but any chance you can give me an example so I know what's eating you?'

Maceo clicked his teeth and let out a sigh. 'I know there are always new challenges to face with being disabled, but I guess I never expected to face them within my own family.'

'I thought your family were supportive?'

'They are. And they couldn't apologise enough.'

'What happened?'

'They put me on the kids' table. They figured it was the best place for the wheelchair to go, but they didn't think about how that would make me feel, or that I was being treated differently as the adult in the wheelchair.'

'But you told them and set it straight?'

'Yes, but it caused the biggest fuss. Furniture had to be moved and the table plan changed, but yes, I didn't get left with the children. But I ended up feeling like the biggest inconvenience for making a fuss, and it was tough and it made me think if this is how things are with my family, who on the whole have been very understanding, then what's it going to be like for the rest of my life? What's it going to be like when accessibility should be a given, but ableism is rife? Because on the whole, people aren't driven to think about things from our point of view and they don't realise we don't always have the energy to make the changes we need.'

'The thing is, you didn't leave it, though, did you? If you can tackle that at the family dinner table, then you'll be able to tackle it everywhere. But don't worry now about the things that *might* happen in the future. Try and tackle one thing at a time.' Harper wasn't speaking from much experience, and she could only imagine how it had made Maceo feel.

'But how can people keep fighting for these things? Especially when we're the ones who are tired from not being given a seat at the table, in every sense. When we're already the ones at a disadvantage because our bodies don't necessarily behave how we'd like them to.'

Harper gazed out of the window for a while, taking in the passing countryside as she considered her answer.

'We do it on the days that we can. We do it with voices. We do it with our strengths. We do it with the resources we do have. One day you're going to be a star rugby player again, only this time in a wheelchair. And I'm going to dance on a stage again, only this time without the use of my legs. If we can build ourselves up after what we've been through, then we can pave the way for others to do the same.'

It was the first time she'd voiced the fact she still wanted to be a dancer. Her life may have altered, but her dream remained the same. She'd thought it would have to change, but then, why should it? She'd had to alter so many things, so why should she change that?

'Do you even like shopping?' she asked, suddenly aware that they weren't heading to where she dreamt of going.

'Avoid it at all costs if I can help it,' Maceo said, his trademark grin back in place.

'Can I change my mind about where we go?'

'I think so. We'll have to check with the driver. What are you thinking?'

'I want to go to a dance school where I'll have a seat at the table.' In the weeks since her accident, she'd halved her ambitions.

They weren't about being the star of a show now, they were about getting her arse from one seat to another without struggling. She wasn't dreaming of being under the spotlight, but of having the strength to pull her full bodyweight up if she should fall. She'd subconsciously put herself at another table without realising that she deserved better. She deserved to be dreaming in the same way she once had. And if she had to start all over again and re-learn everything, but in a different way, then so be it.

'Do you know anywhere?' Harper asked the driver.

'I don't, but I know somewhere that will. Although I don't think they'll be open on a bank holiday, but I can show you where it is,' the driver said.

'Let's go there, then. Shopping will have to wait,' Harper said.

'Yee-haw!' Maceo whooped as if they were off to a rodeo.

The driver took them back the way they had come and Harper's hand found its way to Maceo's to give it a squeeze of thanks. Not in a romantic way, but as a way of acknowledging they were there for each other. Gym buddies during rehab that would become buddies for life.

'Of course!' Maceo said, when they arrived in a car park. 'These guys are bound to know. You normally get referred to them once you're discharged from rehab. They'll have the info and can sort you out with some contacts when they are open.'

Harper wasn't about to join a dancing troupe on stage today. Even though she was improving all the time and was far more capable than when she'd started, she knew it wouldn't be as simple as that. But this was about knowing where to start.

And if there were ways to go about such things, arriving in a limo, with a new friend on hand, seemed like the best way to start.

CHAPTER NINETEEN

JODIE

Three vomiting emojis

Jodie had no idea what message to send her sister when the only true reflection would be three puking emojis. She wrote *Happy Boxing Day!* instead and hoped there wouldn't be any follow-up messages today. She'd missed the one from yesterday and was in danger of missing a whole lot more based on how she was feeling.

She was still in bed, thankful that her usual café duties didn't recommence for a couple of days. The theatre wasn't going to wait, though, and they all needed to leave in about half an hour.

Despite it being late afternoon, Jodie hadn't even managed to venture to the inner pod to find out how the other two were. Nor had she heard any movement.

Every part of her hurt, from her stomach lining to her fingertips. It was as if she'd damaged herself by doing something she couldn't recall. There was a strong possibility that were true, but she didn't remember being anywhere other than inside the flat. Unless they'd gone out and played on some kids' playground equipment and fallen off, it was hard to understand why she hurt this much.

It was once she was halfway out of bed that she remembered. She'd done things, several things, she'd never done in her life. While it had been enjoyable at the time, she wasn't sure that feeling like her body had been split down the middle like a pistachio shell was really the way forward.

With only about quarter of an hour to go before they needed to leave, Jodie crept through the other bedroom and greeted the others, who were already up and in the lounge, before sticking herself under the shower in the hope it would help her feel human again. It didn't, but at least she was able to clear the sleep from her eyes.

'Do you feel as bad as I do?' Jodie asked when she emerged from the bathroom.

'We've had a little pick-me-up, darling. Only way to get through the performance after a heavy one. Care to have a little sniff?' Jasper asked.

Jodie wondered at what stage they'd become so casual about their drug use. She'd only have to say something to the director and they'd be replaced. But, right now, that included her.

'No. I think I'll go for some conventional paracetamol.'

'If you're sure, but if you're struggling, you let me know.'

Jodie did struggle for the rest of the day. She felt like a husk of herself. As if her innards had been taken out and rearranged and the pain was an agony too far. If it hadn't been self-inflicted, she'd be tempted to call off sick, but it was too late to arrange a replacement.

It was worse while she was on stage. She pranced and sang, but it came with an impossible pain, as if her muscles had been tangled.

It was when they were enjoying a momentary pause in the wings that Jasper offered again. This time she was in too much pain to say no. She didn't want to let anyone down, and if this would prevent that, then so be it.

The loneliness that had been creeping in gradually had come and taken its place beside her. With every pain that gripped her insides, she wondered who would care if she were to collapse now. Who would notice? Because there was something very telling in the way her family had reacted in the aftermath of Harper's accident. Were they even aware that she existed any more? The invites to come and see the pantomime were still unanswered. Sometimes people didn't collapse in an obvious way that would require immediate medical attention. Sometimes people slipped away little by little in a way that could easily go unnoticed.

Sniff. Sniff. A quick shift from one nostril to the other. Only the shift was more significant than that. It was from one way of life to another. It was the difference between a one-off and a habit. The change was instant, as if popping candy was dancing along every nerve ending she possessed. It got her through the rest of the performance and all the way to bedtime without noticing the pain. Without noticing too much of anything.

Only, by the morning Jodie was a broken shell once again, not knowing how she would get through the day. So when Jasper offered again, she knew she had to say yes, even if it meant whatever money she had been saving would vanish. She'd worry about that another day.

Today, she just needed to feel better.

CHAPTER TWENTY

HARPER

What. A. Year.

Generally, in the time between Christmas and New Year, Harper ended up feeling all philosophical. This year, more so than ever.

Whatever goals she'd drawn up at the end of last year had been well and truly scrapped. Normally, she'd see that as a failure, but this year everything had changed. Things that were beyond her control had occurred and she knew not to blame herself. Yes, she'd been the one dancing across a road when it had happened, but no one there could have predicted the speeding taxi. It had been a freak accident and she wasn't going to spend her days overanalysing something that wasn't going to change.

Instead, she was going to make good on setting new goals and finding new opportunities. The first truly wasn't different to her previous ambitions. She was going to learn how to dance in a chair. She was going to find a group near where she was going to be after her rehabilitation, and she would put in as many hours as possible to get herself on stage again.

As far as she was concerned, she should be at the main table. She was using Maceo's experience as her own analogy and it was giving her the energy to continue dreaming big. If she'd been striving for star roles before, she didn't see why she shouldn't still. Just because she couldn't think of any starring West End roles fulfilled by a wheelchair user, she didn't see why it wasn't possible and why she shouldn't be the one to achieve that. And she was going to use every ounce of her energy to get there.

Whereas sometimes it took lots of time and thought to visualise her goals and ambitions for the year ahead, today it was easy. And while the overall goal might take longer than a year, every day could get her closer to that achievement. She knew from experience that if she broke her fitness goals down into bitesize pieces, it was easier. And soon, a complicated move would become easy if she worked hard.

Once she'd written down her resolutions, she felt better about everything. She knew it wasn't for everyone, but she'd always found they helped give her year some focus, and she was pragmatic about the things she didn't achieve.

But all the items she'd written down in her new diary were examples of her getting ahead of herself. It wouldn't be the first time and it certainly wouldn't be the last. Instead, having written down her goals, she needed to focus on today's meeting. In one week, her period of rehabilitation here would be over. She'd come a long way since she'd first arrived, when even her balance hadn't adjusted to her new set of circumstances. The early days of being unable to transfer herself seemed a long time ago. But despite the definite progress, she still had a way to go.

She had butterflies on another level as she made her way down the hallway to where the multidisciplinary team meeting was taking place. It was funny how the sensation in that area was lessened, but certain things remained the same. Nerves kicking in hadn't changed.

Part of her anxiety was due to her parents' presence. She'd told them about the meeting, but only because she was keeping them up to date on her progress. It hadn't been an invitation, but they'd turned up with the expectation that they should be involved. Harper had worded her desire to go to the meeting alone very carefully.

The thing was, they were talking about buying a house again so they'd be able to live with her and look after her. They'd already been discussing the kind of home they'd have to buy in order to meet her needs. It was a strange new development where they were discussing her without including her in the conversation. In a way, she understood it. She was their child and at last they wanted to look after her, but the whole idea of the rehab programme was to promote an independent life. That's what she wanted and she didn't want her parents to give up the life they were enjoying. Returning to living in a house would be a backwards step for them as well as for her. So, for once, rather than keeping the peace and not saying anything, she'd told them that she needed to do what *she* wanted.

And facing a roomful of clinicians didn't help her nerves. Aden and Yasmine were there, along with everyone else who'd been involved with her care over the past few weeks. Doctor Patel, who'd been her consultant during her stay, led the discussion. It was a bit like attending a parent–teacher meeting in secondary school where everyone gave a short report on how you were getting on and where they saw any progression heading. Aden's report seemed the most important, and everyone listened in.

'Harper's been doing brilliantly with her physical training. She's now independent with transfers from her chair and can get herself from lying to sitting without assistance. I think she'd like to continue improving her own strength levels and I know she's enthusiastic about getting back to her previous role as a dancer and is eager for adapted training.'

'Do you have any recommendations?' Doctor Patel asked.

'I'd like to put her name forward to the Dance Every Body charity to see if they'd agree to a further period of rehabilitation and dance training there. We can then assess any discharge options once that's complete.'

'Where's that?' Harper asked, again feeling left out of the conversation.

'Dance Every Body is a dance school for those with disabilities. It's outside London, near Dartford. You'll only get a place if they have space, but I think it's a really good option. I'll contact them as soon as we're finished, if everyone's happy with that plan?'

Everyone murmured their consent, along with Harper, who also crossed her fingers. It sounded perfect. Continuing her rehabilitation with some dance training involved was exactly what she was hoping for at this stage.

'I'll call them right now,' Aden said, before heading off to his office.

Harper made her way back to her room, twirling the wheelchair slightly, not unlike Maceo had done when she'd first met him. It was strange for him not to be at the meeting when he'd played such a major role in her time here. The three-times-a-week gym sessions had become five, and there wasn't a day that passed without them chatting to each other. His company was one thing she would miss, but they both had goals they needed to go and achieve.

'We're going to head off now,' her mum said, as Harper joined them in her room.

'We want to miss the worst of the traffic,' her dad added.

'Did you hear the plans, then?' Harper wondered if they'd been listening in.

'We know you want to move on without us interfering. We

know we're not clucking hens when it comes to being your parents, but we wanted you to know we'd be there for you if we were ever needed. I know we enjoy the life we have now, but that doesn't mean we wouldn't drop everything if it was necessary. That's why we came. We needed you to know it was an option.'

For a moment, Harper's throat seized as if someone had sealed it closed. Even though they were whimsical, her parents were there for her and she was sure the same applied to Jodie as well. They just weren't the greatest at demonstrating it at times. 'Thank you,' she managed, in a whisper.

There was a knock on the door, and it was a blessing to have something to distract from the emotion in the room.

Aden ducked his head round the door. 'They have a space for you to do the dance training. I just wanted you to know before I go ahead and finalise all the details.'

'Thank you,' Harper said, a relief washing over her that she hadn't expected. This was it. An opportunity had magicked itself up and it was one she wasn't going to pass up.

'That's amazing news, sweetheart!' her mum exclaimed as both her parents offered their congratulations.

In that moment, she wished Jodie was here. It didn't seem right that she wasn't celebrating with her, but for the first time in her life she'd needed to strike out alone. She'd needed to reduce contact temporarily so she could spread her own wings.

Harper realised she'd not thought about her sister once during the meeting. And this was a clear sign that she'd managed to achieve what she'd set out to do. She just had to hope that Jodie had managed to do the same. Because while she appreciated the current parental support, they needed to make sure they extended the same to her sister.

She sensed that Jodie needed it as much as she did.

CHAPTER TWENTY-ONE

JODIE

Three excited emojis

If an entire day off for Christmas had been exciting, the treat of having New Year's Eve and New Year's Day off her theatre schedule was on another level.

Only, Vince had asked her to do an extra evening shift at the café and she needed the extra income too much to say no. If she'd known how busy it would be, and the kind of customers they'd be dealing with, she wouldn't have been so quick to accept.

'Is it usually this bad?' Jodie asked Antoine.

'You're here for the New Year's special. It's never this hectic usually, but every New Year they flood the place so they can watch the fireworks followed by a late-night kebab.'

The evening shift was proving to be much busier than she was used to. Even the extra pay wasn't going to be enough to make it worthwhile. While she and Antoine were rushed off their feet, Vince didn't do anything to help on the business side of the counter. He was too busy chatting to the customers as if they were long-lost relatives.

'How was your beach trip?' Jodie asked, during a short lull between customers.

'Not the same without you,' Antoine said with a glint in his eyes. 'How were your celebrations?'

'Rubbish. I was encouraged to drink far too much and I'm still paying for it.' She didn't need to go into the details of exactly how much, or what else was involved.

'*Tut tut*... You know, I believe saying no to alcohol is the best way.'

Jodie nodded. She knew Antoine was tee-total and she wished she had joined in with his Christmas tradition instead. She'd be in much less of a mess as a result. She wouldn't be experiencing the itching pain that didn't want to go away.

She'd been about to say something. To admit to what had happened. Maybe even ask for his help, but before she had a chance, the next customer arrived. Then another. The steady stream kept coming for the rest of the shift and by the end of it she'd not managed to say anything before they'd parted ways.

On her way back to the flat, the familiar gnawing feeling was taking over. She'd promised herself that she wouldn't do it any more. That this strange hiatus had driven her to it and she wasn't going to go into the New Year with a newfound addiction. But barely an hour into the start of a new year, that itch was emerging and had to be scratched. Nothing else mattered.

No one was in the flat when she arrived. Jasper and Denna had been heading out to a big party because their plans didn't involve a greasy café shift. They still weren't back. Probably wouldn't be for a few hours yet. But Jasper had left a note on the table for her with a small pouch of what she required. She almost whooped at seeing it, the relief bigger than she was: *Happy New Year, Jo! In case you need to take the edge off! See you next year!!*

If there had been any sense of willpower within her, it spiralled away like a firework ascending into the night air. It couldn't have deserted her quicker if it tried. The answer to her current needs was sitting there on the table, so how could she resist? Even if she wanted to, she was too tired to try. It would help get rid of the itching and pain and would ensure her some sleep.

As ways to see in a new year went, a shift at a greasy café and a sniff of coke weren't things she ever thought she'd opt for. But perhaps because it was easy, it didn't seem like there was much of a decision to make. It was practically made for her. Because that's what often happens when life starts to spiral out of control.

CHAPTER TWENTY-TWO

HARPER

Happy New Year!

Harper usually loved the first day of the year. There was a newness that came with it and the promise of an entire year to enjoy. She saw it as wiping a slate clean and starting over.

But this year, the spring-like feeling had deserted her and instead there was an ominous black cloud. Something was wrong. She had to see her sister.

For a few days now the messages she'd been receiving were nothing other than emojis. Generally, they were three facial expressions that gave very little away. Not that three words divulged much more information, but they'd at least given some small reference as to what was going on in Jodie's life.

Unless she heard anything more in the next few days, Harper was going to make a temporary escape from rehab to work out what was going on. If nothing else, now the six weeks were nearly up, they needed to give up the limited communication. It had given Harper the space she'd hoped for, but it couldn't go on forever.

'Are you okay?' Maceo asked.

They'd convinced Aden to open up the gym for a few hours for anyone who wanted to use it to get over the lull of Christmas. With the bank holidays and various staff having annual leave, it had been a strange week to be in hospital, so Maceo had suggested this to brighten Harper's spirits.

'I've just got a lot on my mind...'

'You still haven't spoken to your sister then?'

Harper spent a moment concentrating on the weight she was lifting. The last thing she needed was to pull a muscle, or worse. 'No. Up until now it felt like the right thing to do, but now my rehab here is coming to an end, I think I need to see her.'

She didn't want to express how strong that need suddenly felt. Like an internal alarm was sounding that she wasn't able to locate.

'Are we going on a road trip, then?'

'Not this time. This is a solo journey.' It wasn't because she didn't want him drawing comparisons, as had been her initial worry. Even though she hadn't told Maceo about her twin at first because she'd not wanted comparisons drawn, that wasn't the reason she wasn't going to invite him along. It was because some moments were personal and it wouldn't be the same if he came along wanting to meet Jodie. That could happen another time.

'But are we going to keep in touch? Once you've moved on.'

'Of course we will. Although I don't have a confirmed date for going yet, but they reckon in about a week.'

'Whenever it is, I'll come and see you once you're settled. Gym buddies for life, remember?'

It added to the sense of things ending, but not necessarily blooming in the way she usually liked to think of at New Year. She had a feeling she wouldn't have minded things blooming with Maceo if they'd met each other at another point in life. But if she wasn't allowing her sister to be a distraction, then she wasn't going to allow a man to be either.

After they'd worked out for an hour and Maceo had headed home, Harper decided waiting was no longer an option.

For the first time in about five and a half weeks, she called her sister. She should have done it before now. She should have called on Christmas Day, when she'd known her sister wouldn't be seeing their parents. But a certain stubbornness had made her stick to her rule because she had vowed to. She wanted to feel as if she was strong enough to face a future without her sister in it. The accident had divided them and an unbreakable bond had been broken. Limiting their contact had been a way of allowing them both to repair.

The sound of ringing droned in Harper's ear. She waited for it to break. To hear her sister saying 'Hello?' at the other end. But nothing interrupted the ringing until it cut off.

Harper tried again.

The same thing happened.

It rang until it cut off. Without knowing what Jodie was up to, she had no idea whether she was just busy, or whether there was cause to be concerned. But the fact she hadn't answered like she usually would was enough to make Harper worry.

For now, all she could do was try again later. Or perhaps get her parents to call, just in case she was keeping to the six-week rule more strictly than Harper was. She might have caved, but Jodie might have opted not to.

One more for luck.

Inevitably, once again there was no reply.

She only had half a week remaining on the intensive rehab they were providing here. Even though they were planning to place her at Dance Every Body for a further period of rehab and the start of dance training, she saw no reason why she shouldn't pop to see Jodie in between finishing her rehab and moving to Dance Every Body. Because their reunion needed to happen. She needed to know if she was okay, and she'd had enough of silly emojis and three-word messages.

It was time to start being sisters again.

CHAPTER TWENTY-THREE

JODIE

Not gonna answer.

Jodie stared at her phone. The message was blunt. *Too* blunt. But when they were supposed to have a limit of three words, it was hard to express that she needed to stick to the six-week plan. It might only be a few extra days, but as soon as Harper heard her voice, she'd know something was wrong. The itching she was trying to ignore was so loud it had become ringing in her ears.

She changed the message to: *At work currently*. It gave a reason for not answering and would mean she could hold off speaking to Harper for now.

It might only be a few days until it came to an end, but Jodie *needed* those days. She needed to get through them without using. All too quickly she'd become dependent on what Jasper was supplying to get through the day. But soon their usual flatmates were going to return and she hoped that would be her escape. When she'd taken up the offer of accommodation, she'd thought she'd be saving money as a result. For the number of nights she was there rent-free, there weren't the usual costs she'd been coping with. But now, what she owed Jasper had quickly spiralled, and all those saved pennies were lost.

Right now, she knew she was inching through each day, a certain agony squeezing its way into her existence. Everything she'd done with ease before now required effort. Every minute representing one where she wanted to give in and take a little something to take the edge off.

'Are you okay?' Antoine asked when she arrived for her shift.

'Why do you ask?' Jodie replied, suddenly self-conscious at the absence of his usual good-morning greeting.

'You look like you've been crying. Your eyes are red.'

'Oh, I'll go and use the bathroom.' Jodie didn't want to give an explanation as to why she was in a state.

Usually when she arrived at the café, she had various duties to carry out. Mundane things like refilling the condiments and folding napkins. But as Vince wasn't around she wasn't going to jump on them to prove how efficient she was. They probably didn't need doing again given the new-year lull. Londoners weren't in London right now, and neither were the tourists.

She glanced in the bathroom mirror and realised Antoine was right. Her eyes were red on more than one level. The whites of her eyes were bloodshot and the bags underneath were red and puffy, as if she'd been sobbing since New Year's Eve. Gathering some tissue and wetting it under the tap, she wiped over her cheeks and eyes in the hope it would improve her appearance. But as it wasn't something external that could be removed, it didn't make much difference.

How could so much change in such a short time? She was not sure what she'd expected life in London to be like, but it certainly wasn't this. And the thing was, she didn't know what to do to make it better. Her parents had chosen who they were supporting and it wasn't her. And the friends she'd made had ulterior motives.

There was a knock at the toilet door.

'Are you okay?' Antoine asked again.

But maybe not all her friends? She should have opted to spend Christmas with Antoine and his flatmates. *He* wanted to know if she was okay, at least.

'No,' she mumbled through the door.

'No one is here. I'll make you pancakes with whipped cream and chocolate sauce. That will help. Then you can tell me what's wrong.'

Even though they really shouldn't have, they flipped the sign on the door to closed. It was safe, because there was no chance of Vince arriving after he'd booked himself a last-minute holiday, declaring he was allergic to this time of year. If anyone came banging on the door, they wouldn't ignore them, but the streets were relatively empty, and they weren't going to actively invite people in.

Jodie was glad of the opportunity to sit down. She'd spent most of her time in London on her feet. Apart from when she was sleeping, her time was filled with either work at the café, or dancing.

'The best pancakes in London. So good I made two lots. Now eat. They'll make you feel better.'

She'd not really felt hungry, but as soon as they were placed on the table her stomach grumbled. Cutting into the American-style pancakes, she realised she'd not been looking after herself particularly well. She'd been so busy trying to get by that she'd forgotten that things like eating were really important.

When she was about halfway through her plateful, Antoine started asking the questions that she knew were waiting. 'What's made you sad?'

'I'm not sad,' she said, defensively.

'Of course you are. I have known you for what... a month or

so? And each day you drag an extra piece of sadness along with you. Before, it wasn't so obvious, but now it leaks from your pores. Even your eyes can't hide it.'

As he said it, Jodie was struck by how empty she was feeling. Antoine's theory was soon proved correct as her eyes started to leak. She hadn't been crying earlier, like he'd thought, but she was now.

'My friend, don't cry. We are here to find the answers.' He passed her a napkin, which she soon smudged with mascara. 'Do you want to tell me about it?'

There were a lot of things Jodie could tell him. There were so many ways she could start her sentence. But for now, she was going to tell him her most recent regret. 'I wish I'd spent Christmas Day with you. I should have taken you up on the offer and then my life wouldn't be quite such a mess.'

'But how so? What happened at Christmas that is making you cry?' Antoine asked, placing a reassuring hand on her forearm.

Jodie didn't have to tell him. She didn't have to admit anything. She could keep it as her dirty little secret, but as she looked into Antoine's calming green eyes, she knew there was no judgement. Only concern. If she was going to confide in anyone, then this was her moment.

'I got offered a pick-me-up, and at the time I was tired and emotional and it seemed like a good idea. Only, I'd not really accounted for the fact that I'd need another pick-me-up and then another.'

'This pick-me-up? You mean drugs?'

Jodie nodded slowly as if she was confessing to herself as well as to Antoine. 'I've always been brought up to be staunchly against them. They weren't in my world before. They've been about more since I moved to London and I've been offered them more than once. For some reason, it seemed like a good idea at the time. But I'd not realised it would come with after-effects.

That I'd be wanting more. Craving it, even. I want it to stop, but I'm struggling already.'

'When did you last use anything?'

'Yesterday. I want to stop, but every time I try, I get offered more and saying no is so hard...' Her temporary flatmates had been encouraging her at every opportunity.

'And the reason you are red-eyed is because today you have had none.'

Jodie nodded. This was the longest she'd managed so far.

'Can you keep away from the people who are offering these things to you?'

'I wish I could.' It was impossible given that she currently lived and worked with them. On the whole, they'd seemed like okay people, but now they were asking if she'd been paid before they were asking how she was. It would seem they needed her to help fund their own habits and she didn't want it to get any worse. The scenario had shifted significantly in a week and now she felt trapped rather than residing with people who wanted to help her out.

'So, let's work out how you can. Remind me who they are, and how you know them? Then we can work out how you break away from them.'

Jodie explained the whole situation. How they were all in the pantomime together and they'd offered her a free place to stay until their flatmates returned. They had seemed like good Samaritans, if a little strange, until things had changed.

'How much longer do you have left at the theatre?' Antoine was sticking to the facts, being pragmatic while she was unable to be.

'Less than two weeks.'

'And after that, will you see them?'

'Not unless we end up working together again.'

'And if you go back to the flat now, will you be able to gather your things?'

Jodie thought about the flat and its strange layout. It was highly likely that Jasper and Denna were still in bed, meaning she couldn't get to her things without risking waking them. Particularly if she was trundling a suitcase through. 'They'll be in bed. I wouldn't be able to without waking them as I have to walk through their bedroom.'

'But you have a key to the flat? You can let yourself in and out?'

Jodie nodded. 'They lent me a key because of my shifts here.'

'Okay, so, when you perform tonight, they will be there with you at the theatre?'

'Yes.'

'And while you are all there, I can use your key and go and get your things?' Antoine raised an eyebrow.

'But you'll be here working?'

'Look how busy we are today. There are no customers to serve. I'll pop out and back before any customers magically appear. Margo will hold the fort.'

Margo, the evening server, was a mother of five children and spoke to Antoine as if he were part of her brood. Jodie had only ever met her fleetingly, but she'd left quite the impression.

'But won't she tell Vince?'

'Margo, like us, is not a fan of Vince. She won't mind if she knows it is to help a friend.'

'Can we keep it between us?' Jodie didn't want anyone else knowing about this. She was hoping to blot out these couple of weeks, and no one would ever need to know. When she met her sister it would be like nothing had happened. Like invisible ink.

'Of course.'

'I don't know where I'll go, though. They've taken any savings I had. I don't have the money to book into a hostel or anywhere else.'

'I can talk to my flatmates and see if we can help out. If not, we can sort out a temporary bed here at the café.'

'But Vince...'

'Vince *Schmince*! He likes to think he has a finger on the pulse of his business, but it's us workers who are in charge here. Especially now he's gone away for a month. I close up each evening. He leaves hours before the shift finishes. And I open up each morning because he doesn't do early. If you come here after the theatre, we can set a bed up each night if necessary. And if you're struggling while those things come out of your system, I can be here to help as needed. We just need to make sure there are no signs that anyone has been staying here overnight.'

'Aren't there cameras? Won't we be seen?'

'The cameras here haven't worked properly for months. Vince is too much of a cheapskate to replace them. He just promoted me to head of security as well as head chef.'

'Are you sure?' Jodie wasn't one hundred per cent certain whether she was asking Antoine if he was sure about risking his job, or if he was sure he wanted to support her through going cold turkey.

'Of course. We need to get you away from these people and make you strong again. I want my bouncy, happy Jodie back.'

She didn't feel like any of those things currently.

'Do you think they will leave you alone at work?' he asked.

Jodie mused for a moment, enjoying another mouthful of pancake. 'If I leave as soon as each performance has finished, hopefully they won't have any chance.' If there was an end-of-run party, she'd give it a miss. Especially given the outcome of the last after-show drinks she'd attended. Or rather hadn't, because they never got that far. It was enough to put her off such occasions for life.

'Then that's what we'll do. Even if it means sleeping here,

you'll have somewhere to stay tonight, a way to get you back on the right path.'

'Thank you,' was all Jodie managed before concentrating solely on the pancake in front of her. Not the itching that was turning into pain. Or the rawness of her lips. Or any of the new sensations that had been joining her as she got closer and closer to withdrawal.

When it actually came to carrying everything out, it was completely terrifying. She went to the theatre as usual, but then had to use as many acting skills off stage as she had on stage. Trying to remain calm while performing was a normal part of the job, but not when those worries weren't about the audience. Instead, they were about whether Antoine was managing to successfully recover her suitcase, and the few items that were scattered around the tiny room, without being discovered.

When she managed to leave without any further questions, she thought the worst was over. That she'd overcome the main obstacle. But now it was the middle of the night and she was lying on a hard floor, the two blankets beneath her providing little comfort. And that wasn't her main worry... It was the concern that at any moment she might get caught. That Vince would suddenly arrive in the middle of the night, or Jasper would work out how easy it would be to find her.

Of course, all of those thoughts were paranoia. She was hidden away. Anyone passing wouldn't see her, but that didn't stop her harnessing every worrying thought strand and weaving them into solid possibilities even though none of them were likely to happen.

And slowly the drugs that were in her system worked their way out of her while she pressed her cheek against the cold concrete tiles and wondered if it would ever end...

CHAPTER TWENTY-FOUR

HARPER

Not long now.

Harper didn't feel like doing much of anything. Not with Jodie being too busy with work to speak to her, but promising she would as soon as the six weeks had come to an end. Harper could count it in hours at this stage rather than minutes. She'd received a longer message than the stated three words explaining she wanted to stick it out because of how busy she was, but was looking forward to a quality catch-up soon.

Something about it didn't seem right. The period of absence had primarily been Harper's idea, to allow her time to adjust to her new circumstances. But now she was in a good place, and desperate to see her sister, she'd thought that reuniting would soon follow. But Jodie had deferred it for the full six weeks and Harper was finding these last days hard to accept.

'Are you ready, ma'am?' Maceo asked from the open doorway.

'I think I'm as ready as I'll ever be. It's hard to tell when you won't let me know where we're going.' Harper should have been delighted by another trip outside the hospital. After all, it could be beyond monotonous as an inpatient for any length of time. Anything to break up the routine should be welcome, but at the same time she'd grown to value that routine. Knowing what was going to happen and when brought certain comforts.

'Somewhere special. You should know that it's always somewhere special.' There was an expression on Maceo's face that was hard to make out, as if every single emotion had arrived at once and none of them were winning.

It made Harper stretch to a grin. She didn't mean to be grumpy with Maceo. It wasn't his fault that her sister hadn't re-established normal communications with her. And it wasn't forever. She only had to get through a few more days.

'Do I get any clues?' she asked, once they were in the limousine again (courtesy of Maceo's organising skills), their chairs carefully stowed away.

She thought about the various trips they'd had over the weeks she'd been here and how much she was going to miss him. This whole period of rehabilitation would have been much harder without his support and, really, she should be the one saying thank you to him.

'Clues would be too easy. I think you should guess.'

Harper groaned. She never liked guessing in case she said something wildly wrong or inappropriate. 'Don't make me guess. In fact, you can't, so it'll remain a mystery until we arrive.'

True to her word, rather than spouting a list of random activities, she enjoyed the views instead. Not that there were many to enjoy at first when the only buildings were industrial and there were no landscapes to spot. The further time when on, the better the view got.

'Fishing?' she said randomly, her curiosity getting the better of her.

'What do you take me for? This is supposed to be a celebration!'

It was a funny thing for him to say when his expression was
one of commiseration. 'So why do you look sad?'

Maceo took his turn to look at the view, taking a big sigh at
the same time. 'Because goodbye has come around all too soon.'
He didn't look at her as he spoke.

'But it's not goodbye. We'll keep in touch. We can still
meet up.'

Harper expected some murmurs of agreement, but Maceo
said nothing.

It made her feel bad. She was so caught up in missing her
sister that until this evening she'd not even considered whether
she'd end up missing Maceo. She'd shared a womb with Jodie,
and then every day since they were born until the accident. Her
short friendship with Maceo didn't even compare to the bond
she shared with her sister.

When the limousine turned in to some grand gates nestled
in a walled garden, Harper began to pay more attention.
Beyond the gates, along a gravel driveway, was a once grand
house that was now a boutique hotel. At least, that's what the
sign outside said.

'What are we doing here?' Harper asked, still uncertain.
She knew she should be happy, but it looked so posh she
already felt out of place and she hadn't even left the car.

'I'll tell you when we're outside and are by ourselves.'
Maceo took a considered glace towards the driver.

It only served to make Harper more uncomfortable. What
was it he couldn't say in front of the driver?

There were a few minutes of awkward silence while their
chairs were unloaded and moved into position.

'I'll be waiting in the car park. Just call me when you want
me to pick you both up,' the driver said.

'Thanks,' Maceo replied.

The vehicle moved off, and they found themselves on the gravel path, which wasn't the easiest to traverse. Harper was still none the wiser as to what they were doing here.

'Are you going to tell me, then?' Harper said, getting impatient. She didn't like not knowing.

'Follow me,' he responded.

She didn't have much choice. The only other option was to go and locate the driver in the car park, but as she didn't want to be rude and they'd have to leave together, she went ahead and followed.

Even though the hotel was old, it was surprisingly accessible, other than the gravel. It made Harper wonder if Maceo had been before. Everywhere they'd visited so far had provided things like ramps, which had made it easier and put her at ease. She wasn't at ease here, though, because she didn't know what they were doing here. But surely it couldn't be anything terrible? Not in such nice surroundings.

Once they were in the foyer, Maceo did one of his familiar turns that was more of a twirl. It came with a smile that provided instant relief because it meant he was acting naturally once more.

'Tonight, I've brought you for a date. A proper one. Because life is short. You and I should know that more than anyone else. We've both been far too close to nearly not being here. And I've waited. And held off. And finally I decided if I don't do it now, then when? If I don't let you know how I truly feel, there's every chance that opportunity will pass me by. And I want to remain friends, I truly do, but I can't pretend that I don't desire something more than that. So we're here for a romantic dinner for two. And if you end up never wanting to see me again, then I apologise. But I couldn't let you move on without making my feelings known.'

A beat of silence followed. Because it wasn't just them in the foyer. There were the receptionists waiting at the desk and hotel guests passing through. And Harper didn't know where to look or how to respond. Because she wasn't elated like she should be. She wasn't filled with joy like so many others would be in this scenario.

Those feelings were absent because a hundred other trivial thoughts were blocking them. Such as wishing she'd worn something other than her joggers. And that she'd asked for clues because she needed them, because the last thing she needed right now was a curveball and that's what this was. And how was her sister? Because really that was all she was able to think about right now. Her thoughts blasted away inside her as if she had a thousand tabs open.

'We can go home now if you like?' Maceo turned to wheel himself away at her stunned silence.

'Let me use the restroom. Then we can have dinner,' Harper said, knowing it wasn't the kind of response he was after.

Harper quickly worked out where she needed to go and didn't wait for a response. She needed a minute alone. Maceo's declaration of wanting to turn their friendship into something more couldn't have come at a worse time. A goodbye dinner as friends would have been fine. It's what she'd expected. But not at a fancy hotel. She'd expected to be at some burger joint, having fun, laughing, wishing each other well and making plans to meet up in the future. Rather than feeling romanced, it was as if someone had put a huge rock on her shoulder, and it was getting heavier by the second.

Right now she wished she had Yasmine on speed-dial. What would she say to all this? What would she make of it? She would probably have seen it coming and, as they weren't friends, Harper couldn't be mad at her for not letting her know. Because what Harper had hoped would be a lifelong friendship with Maceo had shifted into something awkward, and she now had to go and sit at a table with him and tell him she didn't feel the same way. He was gorgeous. She liked everything about him, but if this was a chess game, he'd played his move out of sync. Now was not the right time for the endgame.

When she finally braved returning to the foyer, a member of staff was waiting for her. Maceo wasn't in sight.

'Would you like to follow me, madam? I'll take you to your table.'

The waiter started to walk and Harper had to follow, figuring that once again she didn't have much choice in the matter.

The corridors were wide and they passed what looked like the dining room, only for Harper to be led further towards the back of the hotel out to the gardens.

'Your companion is waiting,' the gentleman said, gesturing in Maceo's direction.

It was January. It was freezing outside. But there was Maceo at a table for two that had heaters beside it and a box filled with blankets. On the table were flowers and there was a space for her to wheel herself into so she'd be opposite him, looking into his eyes.

There was a huge temptation to reverse. To move herself out of this situation. But if she did that, it would mean losing a friend. Perhaps she'd lose him anyway if he didn't recover from her telling him this wasn't what she wanted, but at least if she moved forwards, there was a chance they'd be able to hold on to that.

'Have I scared you?' Maceo asked as she approached the table.

Scared was exactly how she was feeling. Scared that her response would lose her a friend. Scared because despite every-thing, her main priority was still her sister. Scared because thoughts of her twin would always come before anything else. 'I'm not sure what I was expecting,' Harper said. 'But this wasn't it.'

'Can we ignore what I said in the foyer? Can we make it just a meal between friends? A goodbye-for-now meal.'

There were a lot of things Harper would have liked to forget. The accident. The time away from her sister. Maceo's confession seemed rather a minor thing to add to the list, but she didn't want to say that for fear of hurting his feelings more than she already had by not mirroring his outpouring of love.

'I'd like that. Honestly, that's what I thought tonight was. I thought we'd be heading to a burger joint and enjoying a few beers and wishing each other well in life.'

'And that's what we are doing. Although, not quite in a burger joint. Because I didn't say anything, right?'

'Can I take your drinks order or do you need more time?' a waitress asked.

'More time, please,' Harper was quick to say, and the waitress went back inside.

Harper took her chance to tell Maceo where she was headed. She'd not wanted to jinx anything until it had all been confirmed.

'They told me where I'm going to be based for the next month. It's in Kent on the outskirts of London where they have a dancing school for disabled dancers. It's the perfect chance for me to retrain and I'm not going to turn it down.'

'That's amazing news!'

It was. She'd wanted to tell him as soon as she knew, but had decided to wait. Now she wished she'd imparted that information before he'd declared he wanted to be more than just friends. 'I'm really pleased. I wanted to be near my sister and they took that into consideration. I won't be in London, but I won't be far away.'

'That's great. It really is.' He sounded anything but positive, though. 'I've got news as well.'

'What is it?'

'I've been offered training as well.'

'Tell me more!'

'I've been offered training for a wheelchair rugby team. Up in Scotland.'

'Seriously? You must be ecstatic. That's what you've been aiming for!' Harper's initial shock was followed by confusion. It *was* what he'd been aiming for. So why wasn't he elated?

'I am pleased. It's just Scotland is a long way from the outskirts of London.'

Harper grabbed a blanket and curled it around herself. If eating outside had been Maceo's idea, he hadn't considered the temperature. 'Why would that worry you?' she said, a tad absent-mindedly.

'Yeah. Why would it?'

'Don't be like that,' Harper said. 'We both have to follow our dreams. What if I'd said yes, I love and adore you? What would you have done? Would you have given up what you've been working towards because I said you could be my boyfriend?'

'I wanted to talk to you about it. I thought maybe we could work something out where we both compromised on location so that we were closer together.'

Harper shook her head. She knew she couldn't stay. She didn't have the stomach for fancy food and she didn't want to go Dutch on a bill that she'd not accounted for. 'I'm going to go.' Harper unravelled herself from the blanket.

'Don't go on my account. Look, I'm sorry.'

Even though she'd managed to cover several feet, Maceo soon caught up.

'Can we go to a burger joint now?' Harper said.

'If that's what you want?'

'And can we clarify that both of us are going to follow our dreams and not compromise anything for each other?'

'Yes.'

Harper didn't want to go into the fact that if they wanted to, they could follow those dreams *and* be a couple, just in case it gave Maceo some kind of false hope. Nothing came before dancing and her sister, and he seemed to have not realised that. Candlelit suppers were never going to win her over. She wasn't sure anything was. Because a relationship hadn't even been a consideration for her. She'd thought she'd made herself clear. He might be cute, but love wasn't on her agenda. She wasn't in the headspace to fall head over heels like he seemed to have done.

Her only focus was firstly, recovering, and secondly, being reunited with Jodie. Because right now, to her, that was all that mattered.

CHAPTER TWENTY-FIVE

JODIE

I. Can't. Wait.

It was on the third night of sleeping on the café floor that Jodie started to sense a change. The jitters had ebbed away, and the strange aches had started to subside. Antoine had stayed with her on the first night, staying awake to keep an eye on her. But the past two she'd managed alone.

Jasper had directed some snide comments her way at the theatre, but as she had paid him what she owed him and said a place had come up without giving him the actual details, he'd not remarked further and she was hoping it would stay that way for the last few performances.

Now she was trying to focus on securing the next job. The one that would take her away from this particular cast and further her career. It was just a shame she hadn't got round to it sooner because many of the new start-up shows had their casts in place.

So she was auditioning for whatever bit parts she was able to with her current timetable meaning she was only able to attend morning auditions. Today, it was for a chewing gum advert. It was only a day's work, but the pay was reasonable if she got the gig.

'Did you give your teeth an extra brush this morning?' Antoine asked as she got in his car.

Not only was he making sure she successfully detoxed, he'd also offered to give her a lift to her audition. He was one of very few people she knew who owned a car in London. The transport system was so good and the traffic could be mega that many opted not to have one. But this particular appointment was between two Tube stations that were difficult to get to and involved at least three changes. Antoine's offer of a lift had been impossible to turn down, especially as she wanted to arrive at the audition unflustered.

'I even flossed.' Jodie smiled her best toothy grin to prove as much.

'Perfect. I'll drive around and find somewhere to stop. Give me a call once you're finished.'

'Thanks.' Jodie leant across and settled a kiss on his cheek, wondering when she'd be brave enough to land one on his lips. Now wasn't the time to get distracted, though. She needed to focus.

'Go into that room and line up against the wall,' the receptionist said after she'd given her name.

There were about twenty others already there, duly lined up by the wall in the conference room, each a metre or two apart. It looked like they were waiting for a sergeant major, not an audition. Having no experience of auditioning for ads, Jodie had no idea if this was the norm, but none of the other candidates seemed to be surprised by the format.

A few others entered and did the same and it wasn't long before three people who'd announced they were looking for the 'perfect tooth role model' started working their way around the room. Unlike her usual auditions that involved performing a dance and reading lines, this one seemed to generally involve standing there and having various aspects of her aesthetic assessed. Which went as far as comparing her teeth to a colour chart to grade their whiteness.

It annoyed Jodie that this was how they were being chosen. It wasn't on their ability to promote a product, but how well they fitted the criteria that had been set out.

'Big smile for us,' one of the trio said, wielding a camera in her direction.

She did so automatically, even though she'd decided she wasn't going to do the job, even if she got it. They were dismissed with promises that they'd be in touch with the successful client. Jodie didn't call Antoine straightaway. Instead, she took a moment to hide in the shadow of the tall building they'd been in.

This wasn't rock bottom. She was a long way away from that, but equally she was questioning why she was here. She'd seen her initial theatre role as a launch pad. The first of many great roles that would improve with each production she was involved in. It wasn't supposed to be going in reverse. This was the pits compared to what she'd been imagining.

'All right, Jo?' an all too familiar voice hissed. Only one person in London had shortened her name to that.

A cold chill ran through Jodie as she turned to see Jasper.

'What are you doing here?' she said, already regretting not calling Antoine as soon as she'd left the building.

'You didn't think you could get away from me that easily, did you?'

Jodie glanced around, more aware of her surroundings now than she had been. The only way out was forwards, and Jasper was blocking that direction. 'How did you know I was here?'

'Small world, theatre land, innit?' he said.

As he said it, Jodie spotted Denna across the road. Had she

been in the audition? She'd been too indignant over the whole process to pay attention to every single candidate.

'I guess so...' she said, uncertain of how worried she should be.

'Oh, I think you still owe us some money.' Jasper laughed.

'I don't,' she said, trying to get past him, back onto the streets of London where she could merge into a crowd. Away from him. So much for thinking she'd made some friends.

Jasper blocked her way. 'Oh, but you do. The lodgings. The extras. It all adds up.' There was a sinister edge to his voice that she'd never heard before.

'I need to go,' she said, before barging past him.

His shoulder knocked into her, and she winced, but she ran as soon as she had a clear path.

'Always knew you were a *biatch*,' Jasper shouted after her.

She almost stumbled over the bonnet of Antoine's car, which wasn't parked as such, but had its engine idling in the next side street.

Jodie dived into the passenger seat as if it were a getaway vehicle. She wondered if he'd witnessed the whole thing, but as she glanced back it was apparent he wouldn't have been able to see.

'Are you okay?'

Shaking her head, Jodie only managed a couple of words. 'Just drive, please.'

She took a moment to steady her laboured breathing. The knock to her chest along with the whole encounter had winded her. As she tried to draw breath, it was as if her body wasn't able to follow the command for long enough so she was only sipping in air, and sips weren't enough.

'What happened?' Antoine asked as he obliged in his role of getaway driver.

They travelled several blocks before Jodie answered. She

was too busy concentrating on whether Jasper and Denna were following. 'It was Jasper. Saying I owed him still.'

At saying it aloud, Jodie burst into tears, a new fear that she'd never be rid of them starting to take over. London could be a scary enough place as it was without a reason to look over her shoulder.

'This is not right. How did they know you were here?'

Jodie shrugged. At a guess, Denna had been in the audition as well and had let Jasper know, but she couldn't recall seeing her to be certain of that. What worried her was that it was something more sinister. That they knew she was staying at the café and had followed her. She had to hope not, because the last thing she needed was them turning up at her other workplace. Especially now it was the only job she had left.

Because even though tonight was finale night, Jodie knew she wasn't going. They'd cope without one member of the chorus. Jodie wanted to ensure she never saw Jasper and Denna again.

'I'll stay at the café tonight,' Antoine said.

He must have spotted the fear on her face; her relief at his offer must have been obvious.

'I'm going to call in sick to the theatre.' Because if Jasper was willing to threaten her in broad daylight on a London street, there was no telling what he might do in the dark wings of a theatre.

And she really didn't want to find out.

CHAPTER TWENTY-SIX

HARPER

See you soon.

Despite her strange evening with Maceo, nothing could dampen Harper's excitement today. It was as if all her Christmases had come at once, which in a way they had.

Her parents had offered to drive her to the next stage of her rehabilitation. They'd been kind enough to sort out the campervan so that they were able to transport her. They'd got beyond the point of seeing her as a fragile egg that could only be handled in certain ways and had realised how well she was doing. So much so that, on their suggestion, they were taking a detour on the way to the dance rehab facility.

Because they'd been wanting to go for ages and were rather at their wits' end with their daughters not communicating fully and using them as the go-betweens, her parents had suggested they take Harper to her sister's final performance.

Harper knew the trip was partly because they'd experienced an unparalleled level of guilt over the past six weeks. A mother and father weren't ever supposed to choose a favourite child. What her parents had faced was an impossible situation where they'd felt they'd needed to channel most of their energy in one direction, while still holding on to their own ambitions. Harper would forever be grateful for their support, but she knew from now on they would be looking to redress the balance with Jodie.

Whatever had gone on, it didn't take away from the fact that she was going to see her sister. The excitement of that thought alone was enough to keep her on a euphoric cloud that took her all the way to London.

Harper didn't mind that they weren't in the West End or that it was the first time she was having to take advantage of allocated disabled seating. That didn't matter when she was going to see her sister on stage. She was going to witness at least one of them living out their dream.

And she had to remind herself that she was reframing her own dream. Over the last six weeks she'd realised it didn't have to be the end for her. In fact, it could be a whole new beginning.

Once her parents were settled in their seats, Harper browsed the programme, looking for her sister's name and any other familiar names or faces.

She didn't stumble across any, but she did find the name Jodie Quinlan in the section under 'Chorus'. Harper ran her finger across the letters as if it would help reconnect them. She did it because she was proud as well. This was another starting block. Jodie could have given up. But she had been brave and continued. She just had to hope that if Jodie spotted them in the audience, it wouldn't put her off her stride.

When the curtains went up, Harper enjoyed the somewhat hilarious pantomime. There was an elf among the performers who was particularly funny. So much so that it was three or four scenes in, with the chorus doing all the bit parts alongside the main performers, before she realised she'd not spotted Jodie on stage once. Still, theatre was always varied and it might be that she was on in the second half, or that she was well disguised in the role she'd taken on. Although, even if she was wearing elf ears and a fake nose, Harper liked to think she'd still recognise her twin sister.

When the curtains went down to signal the end of the first half, Harper hoped her parents had come to the same realisation.

'Do you want anything to drink, love?' her dad asked, up already, and keen to be the first to get to the bar.

'I'm okay, thanks.'

'I'm dying for the loo. Do you need to come?' her mum asked.

'I'm good. I'll wait here.'

She didn't know what to make of her parents not saying anything about Jodie's absence. It was hard to tell if they were beginning to worry as well.

Rather than waiting in the same spot, Harper moved herself along the flat landing at the back of the theatre. She needed to stretch and move as much as the next person.

'God, Jodie, I knew you were off sick, but they didn't say you'd injured yourself.' A sound man broke away from his booth and looked at her in awe.

The audience were beginning to take their seats once more and Harper didn't know where to look or what to say.

'Is Jodie sick?' she asked.

'Oh God, sorry, you must be a relative. She's called in sick today.'

'Do you know why?'

'No, sorry. I don't know anything more.'

'Thanks,' she said before wheeling herself away.

It was the first time she'd been mistaken for her sister since the accident. Before, it had happened all the time, but now there was one striking difference. She didn't want to have to explain they were twins if he hadn't worked it out so letting him think what he liked seemed like the better option. An announcement ushered everyone back to their seats and the curtains were already up by the time her parents were back in their seats.

She should let them know that Jodie wasn't here. That after weeks of waiting they weren't about to see their daughter on stage. But she wasn't about to start whispering when she didn't have any other information. She didn't know why Jodie was unwell, or whereabouts they'd find her.

Instead, Harper spent the rest of the show mulling over the fact that if the sound man's reaction was anything to go by, no one here knew Jodie had an identical twin sister. She wasn't about to introduce herself to the cast, knowing that their connection was immediately obvious.

The disappointment of not seeing her twin was significant, but just because she'd not seen her on stage didn't mean that Harper wasn't ever going to see her again. But when her parents said they didn't have a current address and there wasn't the time to seek her out when they needed to deliver Harper to her new placement before midnight as promised, she couldn't help but be devastated.

She'd thought the wait was over, but it wasn't going to end today.

CHAPTER TWENTY-SEVEN

JODIE

Even though it had happened the day before, Jodie hadn't been able to shake the run-in with Jasper out of her system. It was now the early hours of the morning, and she was still fretting about it. By now they would have finished their final performance and be out somewhere celebrating the occasion, probably not giving her another thought.

That didn't stop her from keeping one eye on the door of the café. She was certain they knew where she worked – she'd mentioned it enough times. So if they were intent on following her, there was every chance they'd turn up here. And while they probably hadn't figured out she was staying here at night, she was still paranoid that they'd arrive when she least expected them to.

Unlike her, Antoine was managing to sleep soundly, with his snoring as proof. He only had a sleeping bag separating him from the hard floor, but that hadn't stopped him from readily falling into a deep slumber. When she wasn't looking at the door, she kept staring at him, deeply jealous of the rest he was getting. Enjoying his beautiful motionless face, his dark eyelashes fluttering every now and again. After a couple of hours of her staring at him, Antoine jolted awake.

'Can't you sleep?' he asked, alert again in nanoseconds.

Jodie shook her head. 'Today has left me feeling unsettled. I just keep expecting them to turn up.'

'Why didn't you say? We could have asked my flatmates or slept in my car so we were far from here.' He pushed himself so he was half upright, and Jodie couldn't remember ever being this close to him.

Part of her felt that if she curled up into him, all would be right with the world. He'd done so much for her this past week.

'But what about your job? You need to be nearby to start work in the morning.'

Antoine shrugged his free shoulder. 'It's not a job I love. I'm sure I don't need to tell you, but Vince, he's not a nice boss.'

'But you need the money?'

'And restaurants need chefs and there's an endless number of vacancies for what I do in London. I liked this because of the location and the people I've been working with.' Antoine lifted her chin with a single finger as he said it and she realised he meant her.

'But... I'm not who I was. So much has happened...'

Antoine had seen her at her weakest, and although she'd not worked with him long, she wasn't sure how she would have got through this period without him there as a constant.

'Shush, my friend.' Rather than trying to take advantage of the moment, Antoine pressed his lips gently to her forehead. 'We do not need to chalk our mistakes up against the wall so we can stare at them. We should draw them on the ground so the rain can wash them away.'

Jodie rested in that position for a while, thankful he hadn't tried it on so she didn't end up regretting something else. 'That sounds very wise.'

'Of course it is. Head chefs are the wisest people you'll ever meet.' He offered another sweet smile that made her insides melt. 'Do you want to go to the car? We can sleep there if you aren't going to be able to sleep here.'

Jodie wasn't sure what she wanted. Part of her wanted to give in to any desire she had for Antoine here on the café floor. Part of her wanted to call Jasper and ask him to end her pain, but she knew she couldn't go back to that.

What she wanted more than anything was to go back to her family home. To sleep in her own bed at her parents' house, but as they didn't own that house any more, it could cause all kinds of problems. 'More than anything I want to sleep. But not on a floor or in a car. I want to sleep on a cosy mattress. It's been too long.'

It had been over a week since she'd started using the café as makeshift accommodation. She'd been longing for a real bed ever since.

'Let's get you a real bed, then.'

'There's no point at the moment. It's three in the morning. I'll just try and sleep again.'

'Here, I'll stay awake and keep watch for now to put your mind at ease. You try and sleep. Tomorrow, we'll find somewhere else to stay.'

Jodie nodded. She'd reached the point of tiredness where she probably wouldn't make much sense, but she tried anyway.

'I know I'm being paranoid, but I'm scared they're going to try to find me.' She'd turned off her phone because she was so convinced there was something yet to come.

'I think, if they were going to come here, they would have done so before now. The main thing you need to concentrate on right now is getting some rest. We'll work out a new plan tomorrow.'

Antoine smoothed her hair. It was hypnotic and she realised

it was a deliberate attempt to help her sleep. It was working. But even as she started to nod off, she wanted to say that it was already tomorrow. They were already in that day and she was no closer to having a plan. Not for anything. Because none of this was working out how she wanted.

CHAPTER TWENTY-EIGHT

HARPER

Try as she might, Harper couldn't get through to Jodie.

Because her parents had planned it as a surprise mission, they didn't seem too concerned to find that Jodie hadn't been on stage that night. Disappointed, yes, but not worried. And the fact that she was unwell had them concluding it was something minor, given that they hadn't heard otherwise.

Harper wasn't that easily reassured, though. This was supposed to be the big reunion. Perhaps, given nothing official had been put in place, she shouldn't be too upset, but she was once again overwhelmed by the feeling that something just wasn't right.

In all their years of dancing, Harper had never known her sister to take a sick day. Come hell or high water she would be on stage, ready to perform. Being at a finale seemed particularly important. After weeks of work, it was often the show that family and friends came to watch (Harper reminded herself that her sister hadn't known they'd be there) and there was often a post-show celebration. That Jodie had not been there for those things didn't sit right with Harper. Her phone wasn't even ringing, which was making Harper worry even more.

'She's not answering her phone. I don't get it,' Harper had said to her mum and dad as they'd travelled towards Dartford.

'If she has a tummy bug, she'll be in bed. Try again in the morning,' her mum had advised.

When she'd arrived late to the rehabilitation facility (as arranged), they'd given her a key to her room and left her to it while her parents vowed to get in touch in the morning, before setting off to find somewhere to park their campervan for the night. It hadn't taken her long to realise this rehab facility wasn't anything like the one she'd previously been at. Her room was pretty much a studio flat with a kitchen so that she could start working towards living independently. None of that mattered on her immediate arrival because she was more concerned with thoughts of Jodie.

She was lost in London. Well, not exactly lost, but lost to Harper in that moment. She had no one else to call or any other contacts and no details of where she was now staying. So other than settling herself in her new room for the night, she didn't know what else to do.

When morning came round, Harper called her, but again to no avail.

Fortunately, it was the weekend, and being on the outskirts of London meant that she was close enough to commute fairly easily. She wasn't concerned about being out and about by herself any more. The issue was where to commute to. She could go to both theatres and see if they had any idea where Jodie was staying, but other than that she had very few ideas. She messaged the couple of people who'd stayed in touch from the original cast they'd been part of, but none of them had any clues.

In the end, Harper headed towards central London and figured if she didn't know any better by the time she was closer, she would proceed to the theatre they were at last night and ask there. Someone might know something.

Being on public transport was a first. Another first she was facing without question; the need to see her sister was greater than her concerns over the tasks she was conquering. If she was a more patient person, someone would have held her hand (metaphorically) and done this with her as part of her rehab. But she wasn't a patient person and she hated the sense of feeling useless. And getting on board the train was simple enough with the help of a member of staff setting down the ramp as needed.

Navigating the Underground was trickier than usual because she didn't even know where the lifts were in some of the stations. Having never needed them, she'd not previously enquired. And there wasn't any headspace for her to be self-conscious when she was this worried about her sister.

Her sister who still wasn't answering the phone.

Her sister who was so poorly she'd been unable to perform on her final night.

Her sister who no one knew how to get hold of.

Her parents clearly weren't as anxious as she was, as last night they'd driven to the coast and had ended up at the Isle of Grain. An hour's drive from London if the traffic was clear. So it was down to Harper to check if her sister was okay.

That was the only thing in the front of her mind as she negotiated lifts and thresholds and steps in places where she didn't want them to be. The distraction was certainly helping.

When she arrived outside the theatre, it was frustrating to find it was closed. Of course – it was a Sunday between shows. What else had she expected? Because even in London the box office wasn't open this early in the day.

Harper let out a groan of frustration and did the only thing she could. She called her sister again. Only this time the outcome was the one she'd been needing since last night.

'Hello?' It was such a massive relief to hear Jodie's voice.

'Oh my, are you okay? I've been trying to get hold of you!'

'Sorry, I had my phone on silent. I'm so glad the six weeks are up!'

'I know! We can talk again.' The relief at hearing Jodie's voice was immense, soothing Harper's concerns in an instant.

'Yeah, I'd been planning to call so we could arrange to meet up.'

'I'm here. In London. We can meet up *today*. I've been dying to see you. I don't ever want to be apart for that long again.'

Harper wanted to reach into her phone to hug her sister. She was already wishing it was a video call so she could see her face.

'You're in London? Whereabouts?'

'Outside the theatre. Mum and Dad brought me to see the show last night and when you weren't here it made me worry. I've been trying to get hold of you ever since. Are you okay?'

'Yes, it was just a twenty-four-hour tummy bug that was poorly timed. Shall I meet you at the South Bank? Further away from the theatre, seeing as it isn't in the greatest area.'

Area-wise, it seemed fine to Harper. No better or worse than any other part of London. She wasn't going to turn down the chance to head to the South Bank, though. It had been one of her favourite places to pop to for dinner when they'd first come here, and the idea of heading somewhere familiar seemed like a good plan.

'Yeah, what time? It'll take me a bit longer than you, remember.'

'Whenever you prefer. Say, midday? We can find some-where nice to eat.'

'Sounds good to me. I can't wait to see you again.'

It was a huge relief to speak to Jodie. Perhaps the feeling that something was wrong would leave Harper, now that they'd made a plan to meet. It had been far too long since they were last in each other's company and she hoped it wouldn't even take a minute to adjust, that Jodie's company would be as easy as it always had been.

Harper's only worry was that the stomach bug was a lie. Having grown up with her sister since they were in the womb together, she'd caught on to when her sister was telling little white lies around the age of three. It wasn't a skill she'd had to put into use much over the years, but every now and then something would crop up, and the telling speed at which Jodie replied would give it away. Rather than talking at her normal pace, she tended to speed up, a bit like when Harper listened to an audiobook with the setting at 1.5. She couldn't have told Harper she'd had a stomach bug any quicker if she'd tried.

So what was it her sister wasn't telling her? She had until lunchtime to wonder what the host of three little emojis had been hiding.

Because while she was no detective, something was *definitely* up.

CHAPTER TWENTY-NINE

JODIE

'Change of plan!' Jodie announced as soon as she was off the phone.

'What's that?' Antoine asked.

'That was Harper, my twin sister. The six weeks is up, and she wants to meet. She's in town.'

'You must meet her then. You must go, right now.'

'She's really here... I can't believe it.'

Just a few days before, she'd not been ready to re-establish contact, wanting to have detoxed before seeing Harper again. With Antoine's help she'd managed it. Suddenly there was a spring in her step because today was a brand-new day.

With Antoine having sent her on her way, Jodie decided to take the time to use some of the local showers. Over the past week, she'd worked out where all the local public facilities were so that she didn't permanently smell like a fry-up. It was a wonder how much the smell lingered, and she'd been doing her best to combat it. Even working at the café for a few hours left a strong permeating odour, so she knew sleeping there was definitely having an effect.

She didn't want that to be the lasting impression she gave

Harper on seeing each other for the first time in six weeks. Smelling like a battered sausage definitely didn't need to be on her list of achievements in the time since they'd last seen one another. Instead, she wanted to give the impression that she had her life together. And she liked to think that on the whole she did. Certainly more so than a few days previous. She'd been in a relatively successful Christmas pantomime. She'd been the understudy, but had never had to step into those shoes. She had other auditions coming up. And she'd managed to step away from a bad situation. But Harper didn't need to know about that. Nor did she need to know that she'd been sleeping on the floor of a café. Not when Antoine was helping her, and tonight, in whatever format he could arrange, she'd be sleeping on a mattress.

Once she'd scrubbed up well enough for her current housing predicament to not be too readily obvious, she set out towards the South Bank. She practically skipped there in her excitement to see Harper. The past few weeks had been so strange without her about. They fulfilled so many roles for each other: friend, confidante, fashion adviser, agony aunt, dance partner and secret keeper, to name a few. So much of who they both were was interwoven with each other. Most people in their lives wouldn't have known one without the other, until recently.

Now there were people who existed in the world who knew her sister, but didn't know her. And equally there were people in Jodie's life who didn't know Harper. It was an odd thing to consider when their lives had previously been intertwined.

If Jodie had been worried about seeing her sister again, that connection helped them both as they spotted each other easily among the crowds. And the bond they had drew a line between them that they both chased until they were in each other's arms. The hug might have taken a slightly different format to how it had before, but the love was the same. The delight at seeing each other would be apparent to anyone who witnessed them holding on to each other for longer than the moment called for.

Jodie didn't want to let go. Not moving would make it last forever. The fear that she'd lost her sister on the night of the accident flooded her mind, and reminded her how lucky they were. And seeing how well and how confident Harper now looked was a reminder of why they'd separated. But now they were together again, Jodie was reluctant to part, especially as her own path hadn't exactly been smooth.

She was seconds away from being in floods of tears. It was so good to hold her sister again and know that her recent worries were a million miles away. She straightened up and reminded herself that she didn't want Harper to know just how bad things had got, and still were to some extent. She'd got clean so that her twin didn't ever have to know.

'It's so good to see you!' Jodie said, because it really was. She didn't need to lie about that.

'Oh my goodness! You don't know how good it is to see you as well. Are you better? The guy I spoke to at the theatre said you were sick so you weren't there for the last performance.'

'It was a twenty-four-hour thing.'

'But you're better?'

Jodie nodded her head. 'And hungry now my appetite's back. Shall we find somewhere to eat?'

The South Bank was its usual hubbub of Londoners who enjoyed this part of the city and tourists who'd come to see what it was all about. With the London Eye and the River Thames as a backdrop along with the Houses of Parliament, it was always suitably impressive and the restaurants and bars along the river-front had a chilled-out vibe.

'You lead the way. You'll know the best places to eat.'

Jodie did after visiting various times in the weeks she'd been here. She also knew the ones with the tastiest, cheapest options. She knew the places that served side dishes large enough to be mains. She'd learnt how to get by on a budget in the metropolis that was London.

They opted for a noodle bar which was both accessible and suitable for anyone on a budget. After ordering, they settled at a table and didn't immediately know what to say to each other. Normally when they were together, the conversation was non-stop.

'How has rehab been? You look like you're doing brilliantly compared to when I last saw you.' Jodie opened with what she hoped was a safe subject.

'It's been intense, a bit like dance training. They had a programme all set out for me, including daily gym sessions.'

There was a beat where Jodie thought her sister was going to expand further, but she said nothing more. 'It's obviously helped.'

'Tell me about you. Tell me about all the fabulous things you've been up to and what you're doing next.'

A server delivered their food and drink at that moment, which gave Jodie the chance to think about what she was going to say. Normally they told each other everything. There was no editing of their life stories when they'd shared every detail with each other. But this was different. They'd not seen each other for six weeks and their only communication had been brief snippets that didn't give any real insight as to what was going on in their lives. Surely anyone having to summarise would only focus on the best bits.

'Well, after you were no longer there, *Gingerbread* nose-dived. So a seasonal opportunity came along in the pantomime and I went for it, resulting in an interesting few weeks. Now it's wound up, I have various other auditions lined up and I'm hoping the right thing comes along.' She didn't have to specify that as yet she hadn't been offered any roles and that they seemed to be few and far between at this time of year.

'Have you made any friends in the new cast?'

'Not in the cast, but in the café I've been working at during lunchtimes. His name's Antoine.' Jodie glanced at the table and realised she'd started blushing.

'Oh my... You didn't express *that* in your short messages. So, is he your boyfriend?'

Jodie had only mentioned him so she didn't have to talk about the cast. She'd not wanted to tell her sister about the people who had pretended to be friends, but had led her into a situation that felt more like a Venus flytrap. Now, instead, she was revealing things that she might not have even admitted to herself.

'No. He's just gone above and beyond to help me out and I think, maybe, now you've mentioned it, I might have a soft spot for him. What about you? There's more to rehab than you're letting on.' Anything to deflect from herself. She didn't want to say much more about the last six weeks. It hadn't exactly been smooth sailing.

'Ah, I should have known I wouldn't be able to keep it from you. They set me up with a gym buddy. His name is Maceo and he's been the biggest support, encouraging me when I've needed encouragement and told me to chill when I've been overdoing it. We just didn't part quite how I wanted to.'

'What happened?'

Harper sighed and played with her noodles for a second. 'He took me to the fanciest hotel I've ever seen to declare his undying love for me. Or something along those lines, even though I'd already pointed out earlier on that romance wasn't what I was looking for.'

'*What?* You've definitely left *that* out of your messages!' Now she didn't feel so bad about not managing to convey everything.

'It's so hard to express much in three words. This needed actual full sentences.'

'You could have squeezed that bit of information in. So, do you feel the same about him? Do I need to buy a hat?'

Harper shook her head vigorously. 'No. He's lovely and he's sweet and he's handsome, but despite all those things, I need to concentrate on continuing to get better. And if I wasn't going to let you distract me from that, then a man was never going to get in the way of it. I'm just hoping he hasn't taken it to heart and we can remain friends.'

'What's happening now that your rehab programme has finished?'

'It's continuing, although now with adapted dance lessons included. I've been offered a month's placement at Dance Every Body.'

'Really? That sounds amazing. I'm so thrilled for you.' When she'd witnessed Harper's accident, she'd never imagined that they would one day be having this kind of conversation. To hear that her sister was going to have the chance to dance again was the best news she'd had since they'd landed their first roles. 'So do we give up our three-word system now and get back to being in touch as usual?'

'My rehabilitation hasn't officially finished yet. Even though physically I'm much better, there'll still be hours of training to complete. They also want to build on the occupational side of things to get me used to independent living. Where I'm staying is more like a studio flat. So it might be wise to keep communication more limited than usual.'

Jodie ate a mouthful of noodles before answering. 'I know you didn't want hours of your time taken up by our usual conversations. So maybe we could make it three sentences instead of just three words.' Even though she wanted the contact with her sister to be re-established, she also didn't want to reveal all her truths, like the fact she'd been sleeping on a café floor. Another month was what she needed to get everything back on track.

'Only if that's okay with you? This placement is a dream for me. I figure I might not be able to follow our original dream in the way I planned to, but that doesn't mean I shouldn't still do what I always hoped to achieve. It's just going to take a bit longer with added effort. That's all.'

Jodie took hold of Harper's hand as if they were on the date they'd both been avoiding. In that moment she didn't want to admit that London wasn't quite turning out to be everything they'd imagined. That none of it was going as well as she'd hoped. 'You'll do it. You'll make it happen. You've always been the one with the best drive. I've really missed you since you've been gone.'

'I've missed you as well, but I think it's been good for me. I've had to spend time adjusting in so many ways and I needed to feel stronger. This next stint is for a month, initially. I'm not far away so I can come and see you more easily if you ever want to. And three sentences rather than three words is a great idea.'

'That sounds good. That way you can let me know when you hear from Maceo. Because it sounds like you definitely will.'

Harper did an eyeroll, and it was nice to see something so familiar that it made Jodie smile.

'I think I'll be getting more updates about Antoine than you'll be getting from me. I'm not considering any relationships. It might be selfish, but the only person on my mind is me.'

'I don't blame you. I've felt like that more than ever this year.'

After that they went down a rabbit hole discussing some of the men who had liked them, but they'd always been too busy with their dance training. Not much had changed on that front. Only everything had.

By the time they'd eaten, and Harper had declared she needed to return to her rehabilitation facility before anyone noticed she'd disappeared, they'd spoken solidly other than their initial hesitation. Jodie realised exactly how much she'd been missing her sister; somehow life didn't tick by in the same way without her by her side.

When it came to saying goodbye, they embraced exactly as they had when they'd been reunited. But the static pause lasted for longer. Jodie wanted to remain in the safety of that embrace for as long as possible.

'I'll message you when I'm back,' Harper said, trying to bring the unnaturally long embrace to an end.

'And we're sticking to three sentences? No phone calls?' Jodie wanted to clarify this. She couldn't work out whether it would be a good or bad thing. She wanted the chance to straighten her life out completely, but she also missed asking her sister for advice.

Harper shrugged. 'I think having some time apart from each other has helped us both. We can manage four more weeks, but maybe we should have a code word in case something happens and we want to break the agreement? There have been times when I've really wanted to talk to you and I wouldn't want that not to be an option.'

'What's the code word going to be then?'

'Something obvious. "Twins" would be too generic.'

Jodie thought for a moment. 'How about "Things are too Tom Hardy"?'

They often chatted about their favourite actor in general conversation, but he'd not been mentioned in all their three-word messages.

Harper smiled. 'Things are *definitely* too Tom Hardy without you about. That's it, then. If either of us starts the message with that, then it means we want to speak to or see each other ASAP.'

It was the strangest of arrangements to be making, but Jodie didn't want to get in the way of Harper's rehabilitation – she'd progressed so much since Jodie had last seen her. And she also needed to secure herself another job and somewhere decent to stay. Hopefully four weeks would give her the time she needed. Because if Harper was managing to retrain, then there was far more hope of their future being together in the same vicinity. And knowing this was only short-term was manageable. Any longer and it might break them both.

Because things were definitely too Tom Hardy. But neither of them wanted to say that out loud yet, neither of them ready to admit defeat. They were both on a quest to prove themselves capable of independence, even if that went against the grain of everything they knew.

Four more weeks should be simple. Four weeks wasn't long at all. Four weeks was enough for everything to change.

CHAPTER THIRTY

HARPER

When Harper returned to the new rehab facility it was with the relief that she'd finally seen her sister.

They'd been apart too long. She'd never previously spent a day without her sister, so six weeks had felt like a lifetime. And after the scare of her not being at the pantomime finale and being unable to get hold of her, it was more than a comfort to see her and know that she, on the whole, seemed okay. There had been times when she'd wondered if everything was all right when Jodie had only been messaging emojis, but it would seem she needn't have worried.

There had been more things she would have liked to know, but for the moment it was enough to have seen Jodie and to have agreed to a greater level of communication over the coming weeks, even if lengthy phone calls were still off the menu for now.

As it was still the weekend, Harper spent her time exploring the facility. On each level there were four studio flats. She imagined they were all identical, but she didn't get a chance to see inside any as there didn't seem to be anyone else about.

Alongside the building of flats was a gym and sports facility, but much like at the previous hospital, not much happened at the weekend unless it was prearranged. The only people around were a couple of security guards on reception who told her that it was an independent facility and many patients went home at weekends and returned on Mondays. They told her where the nearest shop was and what the best local takeaways were.

She made her way to the corner shop as they'd promised it wasn't too far away, and managed to stock up on some basics. On her return, gesturing a thanks to security, she went back to her room.

It was a different experience entirely to the hospital, and she didn't know what to make of the place. It was like she'd turned up to student accommodation, but they'd had no record of her booking so hadn't scheduled staff to be on hand. The absence of people was bizarre, but welcome all the same.

She'd rarely been alone at hospital. Throughout her rehab there had been shared wards to contend with or the various medical checks they liked to carry out. An entire afternoon to herself meant there was only one thing she wanted to do and she planned to relish it in its entirety... she was going to lie on her bed and have a nap.

She'd had a string of restless nights, and now she'd seen that Jodie was okay, she was more than ready to catch up on a few hours' kip. Nothing could be more inviting.

Once she'd managed to get herself onto her bed and tucked under a sheet, her phone started to ring.

It was Maceo.

It had been less than twenty-four hours since she'd left Stoke Mandeville. Less than two days since their disastrous evening out when he'd attempted to woo her and the whole event had made her uncomfortable. She wasn't ready to talk to him yet. If her sister was able to give her space, then he should do the same.

Harper switched her phone to silent and tried not to over-think any of the things that were on her mind. For now, she needed to rest and get ready for the next stage of her life.

The stage where she would learn to dance all over again.

CHAPTER THIRTY-ONE

JODIE

It was so good to see you. I keep smiling when I think about it. Taking that euphoria with me to all my auditions.

Jodie hadn't had evenings to herself for so long she'd forgotten what to do with them. But with the pantomime over, and no other productions currently on the horizon, she had more time to kill.

Rather than doing anything exciting with her time, that evening she was hanging around the café. Partly because Antoine had said she should, and partly because she had nothing better to do that wouldn't cost her money. She wasn't being paid, so she was spending most of her time reading a book and occasionally helping out during busy spells. Fortunately, that didn't tear her away from her novel too often.

In all honesty, she was struggling to concentrate on the words. Instead, thoughts of her sister were distracting her. It had been wonderful to see her and finally be reunited, but Jodie knew she'd presented a facade and she wondered how much longer she could have kept it up in Harper's presence. The 'dream' that they'd always been aiming for still felt very far from her reach, and currently she was only just getting by.

'Are you ready?' Antoine asked, disturbing her reflective mood.

'Ready? It's not closing time yet,' she replied. Antoine had told her he'd sorted somewhere for her to stay and they'd head there after work, but given the café didn't close until midnight she wasn't aware she had to be ready for ten.

'Vince hasn't returned from his holiday yet and he owes me more hours in lieu than I can count. I think we're allowed to close a couple of hours early at our quietest time of year.'

Jodie glanced around to do a headcount of customers, but there were none.

'I'm more than happy to get an early night,' Margo said, already untying her apron.

'So, are you ready?' Antoine asked again.

Jodie shrugged. 'I guess I am in that case.'

She'd been stowing her belongings at the café, and instead of her large suitcase, she had a small overnight bag ready.

'Let's go. I'll see you tomorrow, Margo. We'll be back by three.' Antoine led Jodie by the hand out of the café and into the night.

The action spoke of a change. They'd spent lots of time together as work colleagues and Antoine had helped her get clean of the drugs that Jasper had introduced her to, but that had been out of kindness. He'd been a concerned friend, and even in recent days when he'd stayed overnight in the café to support her, he'd always drawn a line. But now he was holding her hand and walking with her into the night.

'Where are we going?'

He'd said he'd secure a mattress for her. Somewhere comfortable to sleep. But as she'd been busy seeing Harper, and he'd been busy working, she'd not asked for the details yet.

'We are going to go to the place you've said more than once that you wish you'd come to.'

'Brighton?' she said.

Antoine nodded. 'I know you wish you'd come on Christmas Day, so it made me think it would be the best place to spend a night. A reset, if you like?'

Jodie punched the air she was so delighted by the idea. If she'd taken Antoine up on his original invite, then the past few weeks wouldn't have been anywhere near as difficult. If it was possible to cancel out bad life decisions, then that's exactly what she wanted to do.

'Don't you usually sleep in your car when you go there?' Jodie suddenly realised that however fun it sounded, it might not fulfil her wish to sleep on a mattress.

'Not this time. This time I have booked a hotel room.'

Jodie decided not to ask if they would have one bed or two. She knew Antoine and trusted him. If she ever decided that she didn't want to take this shift in dynamics any further, she knew he'd respect that.

So for now, she was going to enjoy turning on the radio and joining in with the songs as Antoine drove them towards their destination.

While she might not be living the dream, she was beginning to realise she was still living. They both were. And that had to count for something.

Because every new day was a chance to start over. Every new day was a chance to wipe the slate clean. And whatever this overnight stay entailed, it was going to be what she wanted. Not something she'd been trapped into doing, like when she'd unwrapped a present designed to create a habit. She was going to make sure she was never in that position again.

CHAPTER THIRTY-TWO

HARPER

This place is so quiet compared to my weeks at the rehabilitation unit. It was nice at first, but I don't think that feeling will last. Hopefully now the weekend's over it will start to get busier.

It had been less than twenty-four hours since she'd seen her sister, but already Harper missed Jodie.

Jodie and Harper. Harper and Jodie.

They were like bookends, and now they'd been reunited it felt like they should be together again on a more permanent basis. Life had been out of sync without Jodie around, and Harper had been living for the end of the six weeks when they'd be reunited and continue as planned. Of course, life didn't always work out like that, and she'd been the one to get them to agree to another four weeks apart.

Even though it had been her idea, she still felt hollow.

Perhaps it was because she was in a new place where no one was familiar. Or maybe it was because, as yet, she didn't have any kind of routine. But perhaps it was because of what had happened with Maceo; somehow she felt like she'd lost the main friend she'd gained during this process.

There were so many things that could explain the hollowness she was feeling, but for some reason Harper felt it was connected to her sister. That should probably be no surprise, given that they'd come together for a short time, but were now apart again. But it was hard to work out why she was left so bereft having adapted so well over the weeks.

Instead of lingering on that thought, Harper was trying to get into the swing of things here. The structure was similar to her course at university – they offered a range of classes and lessons at set times. There were up to four sessions a day and there was a mix of people in each class.

'Are you new?' a girl lining up next to her asked.

'Yes,' Jodie said, offering a smile.

'It's exactly like dance school. Everyone's in competition with each other to make sure they're the best. Let's not do that. Let's be friends. I'm Anna.'

'I'm Harper. It's nice to meet you. Are you staying here as well?'

'No, the residency is only ever for four weeks. I was discharged nearly six months ago, but it's not far for me to come so I've carried on with paid lessons.'

Their small talk was soon interrupted by the instructor wanting to start the class. Her name was Tatiana and she was also in a wheelchair. It made a refreshing change to be taught by someone in the same situation, and soon the hour was over and it was time to break ahead of the next session.

Anna had to head off and made promises of seeing Harper the following week. It had only provided a brief break from the hollow sensation that wasn't shifting.

Once the day was over and she'd completed all her classes with fairly minimal interaction with the other people there, she decided it was time to face something, or rather someone, she'd been avoiding. It was time to call Maceo.

She'd much rather have called her sister to work out why she was feeling unsettled. Especially given that she shouldn't be now that they'd seen each other. But for now, calling her friend would have to do. Because she was beginning to realise that a friend to depend on was important. And as many of the girls here didn't seem to want to even talk, she was going to work on re-establishing the most important friendship she'd discovered since having her accident.

She was going to wave an olive branch and hope it did the trick.

CHAPTER THIRTY-THREE

JODIE

I have a day off! They're so rare that I've treated myself to a day trip to the beach. Can't remember when I last saw sand!

Despite thinking that Antoine had been getting ready to make his move, it had been a pleasant surprise when they'd checked in to a twin room. The relief had partly been down to how much she needed a good night's sleep. Staying in the café had meant she was subjected to uncomfortable sleeping angles, strange noises and the ever-present fear of getting caught.

Getting an entire, unbroken night was a gift that left her wanting more. That desire was foiled by the fact they had to check out by ten and needed to be back in London by three. Still, having a fry-up at the hotel and a walk on the beach made stepping back towards reality that much easier.

'Thank you for all of this,' Jodie said, as they strode along the pebble beach. Not quite the sand she'd told her sister about. 'I love London, but I think I've got caught up in what they refer to as the rat race. It's as if work and money have become more important than anything else.'

'You're definitely smiling more than you have for a while. I think the combination of coming here and seeing your sister has done you the world of good.'

'I think what I needed was to see her. And I think I needed this to remind me London isn't the be all and end all.'

Antoine intertwined his fingers with hers and she found she was drawn to the gesture. 'Sometimes you don't find happiness in the place where you are, but rather the person you're with.'

The long pebble beach stretched out before them with only the antique Brighton pier providing an interruption. Its long legs cutting into the sea, but creating a postcard-perfect view. It was too early for the rides or the dance hall to be open, but they'd already commented on how it would be lovely to visit again and do it all properly next time round.

With the smell of the sea and the sound of gulls surrounding them, it was easy to find a slice of happiness. But was it really Antoine who was the cause of it? She wouldn't be here without him. She might still be stuck in that sub-chamber of a bedroom if he'd not listened when she'd asked for help. 'I think you might be right.'

Antoine placed a light kiss on her forehead and, once again, he didn't try to push it any further. He was a perfect gentleman compared to so many of the other boys she'd known. 'We'd best set off soon. The traffic tends to be lighter at lunchtime.'

'Can we stay for a few more minutes?' Jodie realised she sounded like a spoilt child not wanting to end their time in the playground, but who knew when she'd next see the sea. She didn't want this contented bubble to burst because what she was going back to wasn't as rosy as this.

But there was a work shift waiting at the café for Antoine and auditions she needed to attend if she had any chance of pursuing her dream.

'A few more minutes. If you insist,' Antoine said, staring right into her eyes.

It was a stare that melted her, and so she was the one who placed her lips on his, hoping the response would be positive.

She was in no doubt that it was when the few extra minutes they'd agreed on was filled with that one kiss. Jodie wasn't sure she even breathed as she enjoyed the most perfect meeting of lips in her life.

'I'm sorry,' Antoine said. 'I do not want to rush anything. I wanted to wait for the perfect moment to kiss you, and I think that I found it. But we must not rush these things.'

'Is it time to go home?' Jodie thought she sounded like she was in the cast of *The Wizard of Oz*. The fantasy had come to an end. London was waiting and she was beginning to fear it as a place where everyone was not what they seemed.

It made her want to stay in this perfect moment forever, so she kissed Antoine again, knowing it was the only way to hold off heading back. It might only give her a minute more, but she was going to take it and drive away the ominous feeling in her stomach for as long as possible.

CHAPTER THIRTY-FOUR

HARPER

Loving the classes. Nice to have some routine again. Is your beach trip with your new beau?

For someone who'd wanted to be alone to get on with her recovery, Harper was no longer enjoying being isolated. She was away from her family. Away from her friends. And the accommodation was so deserted that at times it felt as if she were the only one here.

Once the initial assessments had been carried out within the accommodation to make sure she was safe, the only professional input she was receiving was through the dance lessons. She should be glad of that fact. It was why she'd asked to come here and why they'd thought it was the best place for her. In reality, it was beyond amazing to be at this facility as part of her recovery. It wasn't like they were leaving her just to get on with things, but still she felt isolated.

Today that was going to be eased by Maceo's presence. She wasn't one for acting like a damsel in distress, but she'd needed her gym partner to remind her what her motivations were. She wasn't sure why, but it felt like she'd left them at Stoke Mandeville.

'Hey,' Maceo said, when he arrived outside the onsite gym. 'How are you?'

Harper tried to ignore any thoughts about their restaurant encounter. She didn't want that to affect their friendship.

'I've missed you,' she said instead, before worrying about what he might read into that.

'I've missed you too. I hadn't expected to get an invite quite so soon. How have things been going?'

Harper looked around as if someone might unexpectedly appear. 'It's dead here outside of class times. It's so quiet compared to the hospital. I should be glad, really, but I'm missing seeing friends.' She felt as if she was missing a whole lot more besides.

'How did visiting your sister go?'

Harper had filled Maceo in during her hours of torment when Jodie hadn't been on stage, and then when she'd not been able to get hold of her.

'She seemed... well. She's got some auditions lined up.'

'So, what's bothering you?'

It was nice to have someone around who knew something was on her mind.

Harper let out a sigh. 'I'm not sure. She said she had a tummy bug and that's why she wasn't at the show when we went to surprise her.'

'And why's that bothering you?'

'Because I know when my sister's not telling the whole truth. I don't think it was a tummy bug, which begs the question, what was it that stopped her being there?'

'Did you ask her?'

They made their way into the deserted gym and headed towards some of the weight machines ready to start their usual routine.

'Asking her a second time would have been like pointing a finger. She seemed fine otherwise and I didn't want to question it further.'

'But it's bugging you?'

It must be if it had come up in conversation with Maceo. 'It shouldn't because it's trivial, in a way. She didn't feel up to being on stage for whatever reason, but that shouldn't affect either of us now. So I don't know why it's still bothering me. Call it twintuition.'

'Twintuition? Is that a thing?'

'It actually is.' Harper laughed because this wasn't the first time she'd needed to explain the term. 'It's when twins have the ability to know what the other one is thinking or how they're feeling. Things like finishing each other's sentences, for example. There's just sometimes a sense of something that can't be explained.'

'What are you going to do about it?' Maceo moved onto the seat and started doing some bicep reps. It was nice to be in his company and for it to feel more like it had before he'd confessed he wanted more than friendship.

'What would you do if it was one of your siblings?'

Maceo shrugged between reps. 'I think everyone tells little white lies every now and then, especially when they don't think it'll hurt anyone to not know the whole truth. But saying that, I can't think of any good examples.'

Harper joined him on one of the arm machines and carried out ten reps. 'I guess there isn't much I can do other than let her know I'm here if she needs me. I guess really what I need to do is continue to concentrate on my rehabilitation and my dance training. I've been so focussed on them, and for good reason.'

'Your focus has been laser sharp. Don't let that stop now. Remember, you haven't let anything distract you from that.'

Harper wondered if she detected a note of hurt in his voice. Yes, not even his attempts at romance had shifted her focus from her goal. And she wasn't there yet. There was still work to do. So he was right. She shouldn't let niggling worries with no real basis interfere with the remainder of her rehab programme. Instead, she needed to fully embrace these last few weeks and hope at the end of it she was presented with opportunities to further her career.

'You're right. Nothing should distract me.'

She almost added 'not even you', but she didn't want to upset him again. Not when she so appreciated that he'd come to see her when she'd needed his company. That counted for more than she could put into words.

It might even count enough for her to change her mind about them being more than friends. She'd put that to bed, though. Now was not the time to change that status quo.

CHAPTER THIRTY-FIVE

JODIE

Back to reality today. He's not my beau. But maybe...

The difference between Brighton and London was too stark in more ways than one. The weather (now drizzling rain) and the amount of people, for starters. But the main difference was the way in which Antoine was acting. Whereas he'd embraced their kiss in Brighton, in London, on their return, he was reluctant to stand within a metre of her. There was no hand holding, only a frown that she'd never seen before.

On the way back, Jodie had dozed off, the opportunity to catch up on more sleep proving too tempting. When she did wake it was as if the season had changed. They'd parked in one of the spaces allocated for the café as it was one of the few places Antoine could park for free.

Not long afterwards, they were out of the car, Antoine giving her a wide berth. It was hard to work out what had changed, unless she'd drooled really badly and he'd realised she wasn't a beauty twenty-four-seven. Jodie was about to ask him if everything was okay, but she didn't get the chance before spotting what might have been the root cause of the problem. Vince.

He'd not even waited for them to arrive in the café and had instead come out to greet them. Only any greeting was largely missing.

'Boss, how are you?' Antoine said as if they were good pals.

'Not the only one on holiday, apparently,' he said, crossing his arms and widening his stance. They'd have to rugby tackle him if they wanted to get into the café.

'It was only a few hours, boss. It's been so quiet and we were owed the time.'

'Oh, you were *owed* the time, were you? A bit like I was owed being informed of such arrangements. It's a shame. I thought *you* could be trusted. More fool me.' Vince was talking directly to Antoine.

Antoine held his hands together as if he were in prayer. 'It was only this once. It's been a busy time. We need a break as well.'

Vince turned his attention to Jodie briefly, looking her up and down as if she were dirt from his shoe. 'And does your wife know about your break with another member of staff?'

'What?' Jodie said, uncertain she'd heard right.

'His wife. The one who receives the majority of his wages.' Vince's expression turned to bemusement as he took in the pair of them.

Antoine didn't change his prayer pose as he swung round to her. 'I was going to tell you.'

'Your *wife?*' Jodie said, needing some kind of clarification.

She'd been working with Antoine for a couple of months. There had been all sorts of conversations. They'd talked about the places they'd lived. They'd talked about their families. They'd talked about their friends and their hobbies and their favourite foods and all the things in between. At no point had the rather crucial subject of Antoine's wife come up. And there had certainly been plenty of rather crucial moments when it should have. Like before he'd taken her on an overnight trip to Brighton.

'Please, let me explain.' Antoine went to place his hands on Jodie's shoulders, but rather than be pinned to the spot, she moved away.

'Let me get my things,' she said to Vince, who was still posed like a bouncer. She would push past him if she had to.

He yielded and momentarily stepped aside to let her in. Antoine wasn't offered the same courtesy, and Vince barred the entrance again. In all the time she'd worked there she'd never been glad about her boss's attitude, but the few moments of grace this provided were much needed.

She'd kissed a married man. She would have slept with him if she hadn't been so tired. All this time she'd thought his guarded actions were because he didn't want to rush her. Instead, it turned out it was probably his conscience weighing up whether he should cheat; he hadn't been so conscientious to loop her in to the whole picture. Not only that, he'd convinced her that she was okay to take time off work, safe in the knowledge their boss was away. The boss who was standing outside and about to sack them both.

Jodie quickly gathered her things. Most items were in her case, but she'd left a few things out when she'd been taken off on a spontaneous romantic trip. As she zipped the suitcase, errant, uncontrollable tears fell from her eyes.

This whole time Antoine had seemed like a solid friend. He'd been there for her when she'd needed help and had remained on hand, especially since Christmas when everything went wrong. But now there was one major part of that solid friendship missing: trust. Especially given that the friendship had gone further, into what she'd thought was the beginning of a relationship.

'Are you okay?' Vince asked, having temporarily given up guarding the door to check on her.

It only took a moment to wipe the tears away. She didn't want her boss, or likely ex-boss, to know she was crushed. 'I didn't know...'

'I knew he hadn't told you when he asked me not to say anything. I should have said, but I didn't think anything was going on between you two.'

'Will he still be working here?' Jodie wouldn't be able to stay if he was still behind her, working at the grill. She'd be too afraid of any more metaphorical stabs in the back.

'I'm not happy with him, but I do owe him some time. Good chefs can be hard to come by.'

Jodie should have known it would be too much to expect him to be sacked. 'Then I quit,' she said, before he had any opportunity to sack her.

'I understand. I'm sorry.'

Jodie glanced through the café to see Antoine still waiting outside, probably hoping to speak to her.

'It's not your fault,' she said, knowing she was staring at the real culprit.

'I'll give you a reference for any jobs you go for. There'll be plenty of similar roles available.'

'Thanks,' she said half-heartedly, knowing the life of a jobbing waitress wasn't the one she'd been after. Nor was having nowhere to stay or falling into friendships with cheating bastards. 'Can you help me get to the Tube station without having to speak to him?'

Vince nodded in agreement and crossed his arms over his chest again, ready to fulfil his temporary role as bodyguard.

Jodie followed Vince out and avoided looking towards Antoine. The Tube station was a short walk away, so it wouldn't be long before she'd never see his face again.

'Jodie, please let me explain. I haven't seen my wife for many years.'

'I don't think she wants to hear your sad, sorry excuses. Now, if you want to keep your job, go and open up and get the place ready,' Vince said, acting as a shield.

She glanced over her shoulder to see his dejected form heading towards the café. That he wasn't going to run after her and fight for her was further proof that she wasn't the love of his life. Vince walked behind her on the way to the station, glancing behind to make sure Antoine wasn't following them.

'I'm sorry again. You take good care of yourself. Give me a shout any time if you need that reference,' Vince offered, before heading back in the direction of the café.

Jodie remained on the spot for a long time. She had no idea what she was hoping would happen, but anything was better than the reality she was faced with. Even a major pothole would provide her with a better destination than not having one at all.

Rather than stay there long enough that Antoine might find her (not that his figure retreating into the café had indicated that might be on the cards), she took herself to the Circle Line. She could sit on the Tube for a while and decide what to do next.

There were some very obvious options open to her. She could call her parents. They didn't have a home to take her into, but she was sure they'd offer some kind of help. She could take some time, dust herself off and start over. Equally, she could summon her sister. It would only take admitting it was *Too Tom Hardy* in a message. But she'd been so desperate not to admit defeat. She wanted to prove to her family and herself that the dream was possible. She didn't want to admit that she was so far away from it that she wasn't sure if it even existed.

It certainly didn't exist on the Circle Line, where she'd been subjected to bad singers attempting to beg and the body odour of passengers on a level that was enough to make her close to passing out. She'd switched Tubes more than once before having a lightbulb moment. It was a half-baked plan that had Terrible Idea written all over it, but it was all she had, so she got off the Tube at the right stop and hoped for the best.

Over the past week or so she'd learnt that all she needed was a sheltered place to sleep. While she wasn't about to park under a bridge or the like, she did know somewhere that was warm where she'd probably get away with resting her head. It had the added advantage that it wouldn't involve any money that she didn't have. She'd forgotten to ask Vince for the last of her pay and, considering she'd been caught bunking off with the chef, she wasn't sure he'd be sending it her way.

When she arrived, the side door of the theatre was open like she'd hoped, and she slipped in unnoticed. The panto props were now stored away, and the theatre programme had moved on to a series of comedy shows. She knew because there'd been nothing that she'd been able to audition for going forwards.

Knowing the layout of the theatre was a major advantage at this moment. Having spent about six weeks waiting in the wings, it was now easy to navigate the place without much fuss, knowing which directions to go to avoid getting caught. There was no show on tonight because it was a Monday. But the box office was open, operated by a skeleton staff who were still there. As far as she knew, the section of side stage she was heading to wouldn't even be inspected by the cleaners in the morning. Why would they, when as far as they were concerned it was a part of the theatre that went untouched?

Rather than rattling her suitcase along the corridor, she lifted it and made every effort not to make a noise, which wasn't easy while holding all of her possessions. Fortunately, the flooring was designed to absorb sound, and there was barely anyone about to catch her.

Ramming the case in the corner, she cosied up in what was a triangle-shaped space where it wasn't possible to stand upright. She had provisions with her to eat and drink and there was a toilet reserved for performances that she'd already checked was open. She should be able to get there from her camping space undetected when the need occurred.

Jodie made herself comfortable with the use of her coat and a spare cloak that had been hanging on a peg. It was early evening and once she knew the box office was closed, she would have her food and hope for a good night's sleep.

Although any hope was limited. Her gut was churning too much from the events of the day, for a start. She'd not evaluated what was developing with Antoine to any degree. She'd just been going with the flow. He'd seemed like a genuinely nice guy, and after he'd helped her she'd wanted things to progress. She'd thought Brighton was the next stage. He'd offered to pay for the room, after all, and she'd thought his reluctance to take things further was down to him being respectful.

How wrong she'd been. Now she was jobless as a result of his actions. She looked at her silenced phone to see multiple messages from him, all of which she was going to ignore. Instead, she wrote out the Tom Hardy message to her sister, but instead of pressing send, she saved it as a draft.

She might be very close to her version of rock bottom, but she wasn't going to give up yet. She was going to get through tonight and hope that tomorrow would be a brighter day.

CHAPTER THIRTY-SIX

HARPER

Happy for you. I've reconnected with Maceo. Don't want to lose him as a friend.

That night and the next, Maceo stayed overnight in Harper's flat. It was all very platonic – Harper wouldn't have let him stay if she'd been worried about him making any moves. He was staying on the guest sofa bed and there had been no awkward moments over whether their status would change, even though she was beginning to wonder if she'd been too harsh giving him no chance at all. Still, his friendship was what she wanted first and foremost.

This rehab centre seemed to be well run. If she needed any help, there were people on call, but as it was about supported independence, that was exactly what they were letting her get on with. There was no Yasmine here, though, to discuss her woes with, but having Maceo's support helped.

It meant for the time he stayed, she wasn't fixated on something that in reality should have no bearing on her life. She didn't even know why one white lie was bugging her so much.

But as humans, sometimes, given the opportunity, it was possible to think about something so much that it amplified and became much bigger. Bigger than it should be by any measure.

She wished Maceo could stay for longer, but he had his own rugby training to get back to and Harper promised to go and see a match once she'd finished the programme.

'Do you think...?' Maceo started saying as he got ready to leave. 'Never mind.'

Harper could pluck the words he would have said out of the air. It turned out she wasn't the only one with a fixation.

'Let's get you on the rugby field and me on the stage in a professional capacity, then you can ask me that.'

She didn't want to give him too much hope, but then she didn't want him to believe there wasn't any either. Because if she needed him by her side to make the world an easier place to navigate, surely that counted for something?

CHAPTER THIRTY-SEVEN

JODIE

It's funny how theatre can feel like home. Really hoping to land another role soon. Keeping my fingers crossed.

The first night of camping in the theatre went without any hiccups. Jodie even managed to sleep reasonably well.

The second night was a trickier affair. There was a show on, and she didn't want to be discovered by one of the stage hands. Instead, with her luggage hidden as well as possible, she was spending the day out and about.

For most of it she lingered in the galleries of the Natural History Museum. The place was fascinating and she spent time reading each of the information plaques to help pass the time, finding out about Mary Anning and her early discoveries in Dorset. It was nice to actually spend some time being a tourist – ever since she'd arrived in London, she'd been too busy working.

Once the museum had closed and the evening was drawing in, she managed to make a coffee last several more hours than it should, and she purchased some reduced sandwiches for a late-night dinner of sorts.

She just needed to time getting into the theatre perfectly. She planned to head to the public toilets when the show was due to finish and then, once it was busy, make her way to her sleeping nook.

The ushers would be by the side exits, ensuring everyone was filtering out okay, so her path would be relatively clear and she'd be able to tuck herself away unnoticed. That was the plan. Only as soon as she turned the corner, she knew it had been foiled. Even though the show wasn't due to finish for about twenty minutes, the audience was filing out of the theatre.

'Shit,' she said under her breath.

The running time for some shows wasn't accurate. For scripted performances it was always easier to pinpoint when everyone would be finished with their lines, but a comedian didn't always stick to their set and would sometimes wind things up earlier, especially if there were particularly horrid hecklers.

Jodie should have got back earlier, but she'd thought she'd left enough time. She scrambled up the side street where the audience members were pouring out. It wasn't until she was a bit closer that she heard an alarm coming from inside.

'What's going on?' she asked a random stranger about to barge by.

'Bomb scare. We've all been told to get out. You need to head in the other direction, not towards it.'

'Bomb scare?' Jodie repeated. There were always strange occurrences in London, but this was a first for her. In the next few moments, a fleet of different emergency services arrived: the police, a fire engine and a bomb squad van.

Her jaw fell open as she suddenly realised *why* this was happening.

'Why do they think there's a bomb?' Jodie asked another random stranger who was eager to rush away, any thoughts of seeing a comedy act abandoned.

'They've found a case or something. That's what I heard, anyway.'

The woman rushed off while Jodie muttered 'Shit' on repeat without anyone bothering to ask her what the matter was. They were all too busy running away from an explosive device. Her underwear (and other clothing) had never been described as such before. She really had to hope they never would be again.

That wasn't her concern for now, though. She had to work out what to do. Because if the bomb squad were here, did that mean all her worldly possessions were at risk? Would they explode the whole suitcase before working out it was just some-one's wardrobe? Her head was spinning as she pushed against the tide of people to get closer to the door.

She didn't know what she'd say when she got there. It was hard to know how obvious it would be that she'd been sleeping there as well as storing her case. All she could do was go with honesty being the best policy, especially if she wanted it back before this escalated any further.

The problem was that it had already escalated too far for anyone to be happy about the matter. Somehow she doubted she'd be able to get to her bag without being caught or ques-tioned by about one hundred people.

Without formulating a plan, she continued pushing forwards against the tide of movement. All she knew was that she needed to stop them. She would accept any consequences, as long as she wasn't left with nothing. But getting inside wasn't easy when she was working against a constant flow of people, all of them disgruntled and annoyed at her for wanting to go towards the building rather than away.

When she reached the fire door she took hold of it to anchor herself, scared of being washed away. What she'd do to be back at the Natural History Museum with its corners of tranquillity. She'd do anything to be there, only this time she'd bear the inconvenience of lugging her suitcase around with her.

'Hi, Jo,' an all too familiar voice said.

Jodie's head shot up and she quickly let go of the door. 'What are you doing here?' she asked.

'I work here, so that's rather obvious. The question is why are *you* here?' Jasper asked.

It took Jodie a moment to take in the fact he was wearing an usher's uniform. She was too flummoxed to respond with any speed.

'Lost a bag by any chance?' Jasper said with a mischievous grin.

'I–I don't...' Jodie didn't know what to say. She didn't want to outrightly admit it, but she also wanted the situation resolved.

'I thought I recognised it when I saw it.'

'Why didn't you say something?'

Jasper shrugged. 'You've not been about. It didn't make sense that it was yours.'

The crowd had thinned out to nearly nothing. Jodie glanced towards the various emergency vehicles that were now gathered at the front of the building.

'Oh, and it looks like whoever owns the bag might have slept here as well. Do you really have nowhere to stay?'

Jodie's eyes started to well. If things had already been bad, this situation was making everything a whole lot worse.

'Oh, darling. Wait here. I'll go and sort this out.' Jasper headed back inside the theatre with a wave of his arm.

Rather than wait like Jasper had said she should, Jodie managed to follow quietly in his wake, stopping before heading onto the stage area.

'Panic over, everyone. Panic over!' Jasper called.

From the corridor, given the added drama he gave to every word, it was easy to hear him.

'I put out a message to all the cast from the previous show

and the bag belongs to one of them. Silly girl forgot she'd put it there.'

There was a huge sigh of relief from whoever Jasper was talking to. 'So, what's in there?'

'Clothes, I believe. She went travelling after the show and was storing them there. Although, she should have asked, obviously.'

'We need to open it to be one hundred per cent certain.'

'I'll do it, seeing as I'm the one providing the information.'

A short silenced followed, and then the sound of a zip being opened.

Thankfully there wasn't anything in her case that was incriminating in any way, shape or form, unless her dirty clothes counted. She needed to get to a laundrette, and soon.

'See, nothing to worry about. We can call off the troops.'

'Thank God.'

'I'll take this and get it back to its owner.'

Jodie suddenly remembered she wasn't where she said she'd be, and rushed back outside.

'Sorted. The emergency services will be off shortly. One of the duty managers is a bit overzealous with health and safety. Always creates mountains out of molehills.'

'Right,' Jodie said, wondering when he'd hand over her case. She was well and truly ready to scarper. Once again, she was without a destination, but it couldn't be any worse than this.

'So, you're without somewhere to stay again?'

Jodie briefly remembered when she'd been staying in the room above the pub. It hadn't been ideal, but she'd had her own space. Ever since leaving there she'd been put into a position where she wasn't able to afford it any more.

'I'll find something...'

'Still at the café?'

Jodie wanted to get away. She recalled her last run-in with Jasper when he'd told her that she owed him, even though she'd settled up fair and square. She shook her head and held out her hand. If he wasn't automatically handing her suitcase over, perhaps he would with a prompt.

'Come and stay at the flat tonight, then. Denna has moved out so there's a space in my room.'

The emergency vehicles, including the bomb squad van, started to pull away. It gave her a small sense of relief to know that they'd stood down.

'I'm not sure.'

'Oh, come on. Just a place to rest your head. You look like you need it.'

'Gee, thanks. It's just, well, since I last saw you, I've got clean. I don't want that to change.'

'Oh God. I totally understand, and the same here. It was Denna who was the bad influence. Here, take this. We can get a late-night drink and you can decide by the time we're done.'

Jodie took the case. She had the opportunity to run, but where did she have to run to? She could go for one drink and then make her excuses. She didn't know where she would go, but she'd got by so far. She'd manage. She'd find a laundrette to clean her clothes, she'd find somewhere to shower so she could clean herself, and she'd head to all the theatres individually to find out what productions were due to be staged and whether there were any chorus opportunities. She'd even do something similar to Jasper and work as an usher or in the box office if needed. She didn't want to have to call her parents, defeated. Especially when they hadn't been part of her life since Harper's accident.

'Come on, kiddo. You look like you need a drink and a chat,' Jasper said, before leading the way.

Jodie didn't know whether following was foolish or not. When she'd last stayed with him, she'd felt like he was preying on her, trying to get her deeper into an existence she didn't want. But since then, the guy she'd thought was her saviour was in fact a cheating so-and-so.

The lines of any concept of good guys and bad were merging so much that there were no longer categories. Because as far as she could tell, the good didn't exist without the bad, and vice versa. She had to concentrate on finding her own way. And that was particularly difficult when she was feeling more lost than ever.

So letting someone lead the way was the easy option. One that she was too tired to resist.

CHAPTER THIRTY-EIGHT

HARPER

Nothing different occurring here. Classes followed by classes. A bit like our uni course!

Since Maceo's departure, Harper had immersed herself fully in her training. For a while, she'd lost her drive, but talking to Maceo had reminded her why she was here.

If she wanted to be regarded as a professional dancer again, then she needed to commit to it like she had before, and with each lesson she was beginning to realise she needed to find her own groove. There were certain dance moves that weren't possible without the use of two legs, so those moments required some finesse.

In her spare time, when there weren't many people about, she'd taken to re-choreographing the final piece she'd performed as part of her university exam. She knew it off by heart, but how was someone in a wheelchair supposed to perform leaps and pliés? For some moves, she'd been taught alternatives, but they hadn't covered everything a non-disabled dancer could do.

At some point recently she'd realised she couldn't let that

stop her. Nothing should. If a taxi ploughing into her hadn't ended her life, then it shouldn't end her dancing career either. And if she had to adapt pirouettes and pliés, then so be it. Adding a bit of flair was what life was all about. In some ways it reminded her of when she'd first met Maceo. He'd twirled and wheel spun and demonstrated how he'd mastered movement in his wheelchair. Now, she'd done that as well, but needed to take it to the next level. She wanted to be able to do things that would stun and amaze, and would see her take centre stage like she'd always dreamt.

Currently, she was working on putting her wheelchair temporarily into flight. It was only to move from one level to another, but she wanted to have the strength to propel the movement and to also control the whole technique so it was a smooth shift rather than jerky. She knew she was being a perfectionist, but with dance she often had to be, so she was just applying that to what she wanted to achieve.

'You're doing well,' Tatiana, her instructor, said as she joined her in the studio.

'Thanks. I just keep getting stuck on certain elements of the dance.'

'Well, you're experimenting. Not being scared to try new things is a good thing. Remember to pace yourself and you'll have it cracked by this time next week.'

A week seemed too long in Harper's books. She wanted it cracked in the next hour. A week had one hundred and sixty-eight hours. That seemed like way too many. But if she'd learnt anything from the early days of her recovery, it was that some-times the mind wasn't in charge of how things went, the body was. And listening to what it was saying was essential.

'I'm trying to remember to listen to my body. Even the bits I can't feel.'

'Look, we're doing some auditions on Friday evening. You should try out.'

'Really?'

'Yes, the details are on the noticeboard. Check it out and make sure you come along.'

'Thanks,' Harper said, a frisson of excitement running through her. She'd thought auditions were a faraway dream. But here was one just a few days away.

After she'd finished practising, she wheeled herself to the noticeboard to read the details, doing a celebratory twirl on the way. One Maceo would be proud of. It was a dance recital that they were holding, to raise money for the facility. She couldn't think of a better cause or way to start. She just needed to concentrate on perfecting her audition piece.

CHAPTER THIRTY-NINE

JODIE

Sounds like we're both in a state of déjà vu. Continuing on the audition treadmill here. Fingers still crossed.

Could a leopard change its spots? Because Jasper had spent an awful lot of energy trying to convince her that he had.

While they'd been having a drink, she'd felt so comfortable talking to him that she'd confided what had happened with Antoine. The trusty work colleague who turned out to be anything but honourable. And as she'd not spoken to anyone about it since it had happened, it felt good to get it off her chest. She'd not really explored how much she'd been hurt by the whole thing. She knew there were rogues in the world, but she wouldn't have kissed him if she'd known he was one of them.

Jasper in turn confided in her. He'd confessed that he'd finally given in to Denna's advances and when he'd only wanted to do it the one time, she'd gone mad. She'd wanted a full-on relationship and had accused him of only using her to scratch an itch. When he'd said he thought it was the other way round, she'd flipped and he'd not seen her since.

Jodie digested this information over her glass of wine and didn't quite know what to make of it. When she'd stayed with them, they'd both seemed as bad as each other. Like two toddlers whose hyperactivity increased tenfold when they were together. The dynamic of their friendship had come across as toxic without the added complication of taking it further.

With reassurances that he wouldn't get her involved with anything like before, and having offloaded to each other, when the offer of staying was given again, Jodie said yes.

The other options available to her, such as calling her parents or sleeping rough, didn't seem as attractive now she was being offered an alternative that involved a proper mattress on a proper bed in a proper room.

She wasn't entirely sure it was the right decision, but given that her last plan had ended with the bomb squad being called out, she thought perhaps she should chance it. If she was offered anything extra, she had the option to say no. She *would* say no, she corrected herself. Thinking there were other options wasn't helpful.

Unlike the last time, there was no late-night party. There was no raucous singing into the early hours. Instead, after idly watching a film, Jasper suggested they both get to bed. It was just before midnight, but still a reasonable hour based on his previous timetable.

In the morning, he made eggs and bacon, and it was so different to when she'd last been here, it was as if she'd entered a twilight zone.

'What are your plans today?' Jasper asked.

'I need to find myself a new job. Two, if possible.' Considering she'd lost both of her revenue streams, she needed to remedy that as soon as possible. Even if it was a waitressing gig, it would mean she could stay in London.

'I'm going to suggest you leave your suitcase here. Save any further emergencies.'

Jodie smiled, although she wasn't quite ready to laugh about it.

'Here, have Denna's key. Then you can let yourself in. Feel free to stay here again tonight.'

For some reason, the cool metal in the palm of her hand felt like some kind of trap. As if accepting it bound her in some kind of spell. She shook the thought away. It was as silly as thinking that hiding herself away in the wings of a theatre had been a good idea.

'Thanks. I'll see what the day brings.'

After Jasper set off for work, Jodie set off on her own quest. She needed to get a job. Any job. And, being London, there were plenty of choices.

She went to a local library and printed twenty CVs. Rather than hand them out to every café or restaurant that was advertising for staff, she handed them in to theatres in the hope she'd be able to secure something similar to Jasper. It would fill the gap in her dancing career. It was definitely a quieter time of year and wouldn't pick up until March, some of her dancing friends had said. At the end of her traipsing around, she got another reduced-price sandwich.

She sat in Hyde Park to eat it. There was something so valuable about the moments of quiet she sometimes found in the capital city. Sometimes it felt like they shouldn't be possible, but every now and then there was a lull between groups of people and for a second she could imagine it was just her. That this place had lived up to her hopes and dreams. That life hadn't changed in its entirety within weeks of arriving here. That she was cool and calm and had a handle on everything.

It was a surprise to find herself crying. Without anyone to witness her tears, it was easier to give in to the overwhelming sense of failure. *She* wasn't the one who had her life altered to the point she didn't have the use of her legs. *She* didn't have to learn how to do daily tasks in an entirely different way. But her life had altered, and she seemed to be making wrong moves at every turn.

She stared at the silver key to Jasper's place. All her instincts were telling her never to return, even though she desperately needed another night in a proper bed. She should have taken her bag this morning so she didn't need to go back for it. But as it stood, she was no closer to getting another job or a place to stay.

So she was beholden to the key and all it offered. In the end, she returned to the flat and hoped for once she was doing the right thing. Jasper had said he was on a late shift so she didn't wait up.

After settling into bed and resolving to have an early night and to try again in the morning, it was before daybreak that Jasper woke her.

'Oh God, sorry, Jo. Look who's back.'

Jodie had been in a deep sleep, but it didn't take her long to work out it was Denna.

'Yeah, Jo, Jasper said you might be here.'

'I'm in your bed,' Jodie said. She tried to get up, disorientated and weary all at once.

'No, girl. I can sleep on the sofa with Jaspie. You stay here and get your rest.'

Having half got up, Jodie landed back on the bed. She didn't have any idea what the time was, but judging by how tired she was it must be the middle of the night. They left the room before anything more was said.

Too tired to do anything else, she nestled into her pillow and attempted to get back to sleep. She definitely needed more rest, but it was harder to drop off again after her deep sleep had been interrupted. She sensed that her body had sent a shot of adrenaline around it in some kind of fight or flight response when she'd been abruptly woken.

When she did start to drift off, the sound of loud sex taking place in the lounge area was enough to prevent her from falling asleep. It was evidently Denna and Jasper. Which confused her after Jasper had stated he'd only wanted friendship and it was Denna who had wanted more.

And once again, it was a weird hideous torture to be stuck in this flat. She wasn't in the antechamber bedroom, but the only way out was to drag her suitcase through the lounge that was currently in use. If she did that, they'd probably think it was because she wanted to join in. And she definitely didn't.

She'd just rather be anywhere else.

CHAPTER FORTY

HARPER

Looks like you're not the only one with an audition on the horizon. Only a dance recital fundraiser, but it's a start. And as I need my hands free in order to dance, can you cross your fingers for me as well?

When Harper perfected the jumping move, her own heart did a little jump in the process. It had taken hours upon hours to get to this point, and it felt like a victory on more than one level. Not least because she was planning on including it in her audition piece.

The following few hours were a frustrating combination of hit and miss. A bit like an ice skater doing a particular move, she didn't always land it how she wanted to and sometimes she didn't manage to become airborne. There was a risk that keeping it in the routine might mean it was a flop, but at the same time she wanted to stand out.

She either would or wouldn't, but the hours ebbed away and in no time, the day of the audition came round. After reflecting on how hard she'd been working, Harper had already decided to have the day of the audition as a rest period. She didn't need a last-minute injury or muscle fatigue to get in the way of a spot-on performance. Because that's what she wanted it to be. Nothing less than perfect.

Having a rest period wasn't too hard because it had been a long time since she'd indulged in watching a Netflix series back-to-back. Unlike a movie that would be over in two hours, she managed to fill the day with episode after addictive episode until it was time to get ready.

It had been a long while since she'd put on a costume and done her stage make-up. It was always more exaggerated than the light covering she usually put on each morning. This kind of make-up was designed to emphasize and be picked up by the lighting so that audience members further back would see her features.

As she joined the other girls waiting to audition, she felt a bit silly as none of them had gone to the same level of effort. But she tried not to think about that. Instead, she focussed on going over the routine in her head. She thought about each separate move she needed to execute. She went over them in her head like an inventory – it was essential that no items were forgotten.

When it was her turn to go in front of the audition panel, Harper did so with her head held high. She was proud of herself, however this went. It had taken weeks of hard work to get her to this place. And it hadn't been as easy as one foot in front of the other because she'd had to relearn how to move her body on its new terms. It hadn't been easy, but she was proud to get as far as she had.

She put those thoughts into every move as she danced to 'Dance Monkey' by Tones and I. She didn't think about the fact that this was her first audition in a wheelchair. She didn't consider the fact she couldn't leap through the air in the same way. She focussed on each move with confidence, knowing she'd practised them over and over again. She knew as she transitioned from one move to the next that they would be as perfect as possible in this moment. She wouldn't be able to alter how each one went, in the same way that she couldn't have altered her destiny.

When it came to the leap that she'd been practising on repeat, her heart missed a beat as she lifted into the air... everything seemed to pause, as if the moment was passing in slow motion. And to her great relief, she landed as planned and moved into the next sequence as if it were a breezy doddle that had taken no effort at all.

She tried not to allow her inner triumph affect the rest of the piece, and finally she settled to a joyous bow at the end by folding her body towards her lap. Curtsies were a thing of the past. Bows were the way forward.

The three people on the auditioning panel, including Tatiana, offered a small round of applause that caused another ripple of triumph to run through her. She was certain that kind of response hadn't been offered to everyone coming through the door.

'We're going to put a list of successful names on the board tomorrow,' Tatiana said. 'Keep an eye out for it.'

Tomorrow couldn't come soon enough for Harper. Because she had the distinct impression that tomorrow was when it would all begin. That she was about to start living her dream all over again.

CHAPTER FORTY-ONE

JODIE

Oh my! That's great news! I'm crossing everything for both of us.

Jodie wanted a swift exit. Anyone in this situation would, but so far it wasn't working out like that. At some point Jodie had managed to drift back to sleep, but apparently the unexpected sex session was being followed up with the same performance this morning.

Hiding away and trying to pretend she couldn't hear anything wouldn't have been quite so bad if it hadn't been for the sudden appearance of two blokes she'd never met before.

Of course, the antechamber pod. How could she have forgotten the room that was attached? The one with no alternative exits.

'What's going on?' one of them blurted out as they burst in, clearly only expecting Jasper to be there.

The two tall, wiry figures were only wearing boxers and had brought with them a strong stench of body odour. Jodie didn't really have to clarify – the sound of Denna's orgasm answered his question.

'FFS,' one of them said, as an actual acronym.

'Denna and Jasper,' Jodie said, by way of explanation.

'Who are you?' one of them asked.

It was a reasonable question seeing as she'd not met either of them during her previous stay.

'I'm Jodie. I used to work with both of them, and Jasper offered me a place to stay for a night or two.' She decided not to mention that she'd stayed here over Christmas in case they were completely unaware. That seemed fairly likely given how unreliable the love-making pair were.

'Honestly, I'm so done with all the theatrics. We might all work in theatre, but life isn't a stint on the stage that needs high-level drama all the time.'

The quieter of the two didn't respond. Instead, he made for the door, apparently wanting the whole sex session to be over and done with.

'Get out! Get out. Get out. Get out.' He was shouting as if he'd just cracked and would tolerate no more.

Jodie looked at the other guy, who shrugged before heading through to find out what was going on. Because remaining in bed wasn't helping her, she decided to follow. She didn't want things to get any worse, and hiding away wasn't going to help. Denna was covering her nakedness with the sofa blanket while her clothes were being thrown out into the corridor by the angry flatmate. Jasper had managed to hop into his boxers and was trying to reason with the guy.

Jodie didn't much like Denna – she'd never been particularly thoughtful about how she treated those around her – but Jodie was loath to see a woman in a vulnerable position being treated in such a way.

'What do you think you're doing?' Jodie shouted as if she were harnessing eras of the mistreatment of women as she spoke those words.

The angry flatmate looked at her as if he'd only just woken up, which was entirely possible.

'Go and get those clothes back and let her dress please before you go throwing anything else out.' Jodie hadn't ever heard herself talk so fiercely, but the tone must have been the correct one as the lad was scrambling to collect the clothes again.

Jasper had put his T-shirt on and had gone off towards the kitchen.

'Thanks,' Denna said to Jodie. The blanket she was using to keep herself decent was also coming in handy as a handkerchief, and she wiped away a few tears with the corner. Her retrieved clothes were passed to her and she glanced at them, then looked towards the kitchen with a hurt expression.

Jodie might have been kept up and then woken up in the worst way possible, but she still felt sorry for Denna. What a shitty position for her to find herself in.

'Go and use the bathroom,' Jodie suggested. 'I'll get you a drink.'

'Don't take long,' the other flatmate said. 'Some of us need to get to work.'

'Give her a break,' Jodie snapped. 'Your friend here just nearly shoved her out naked. Maybe don't complain about the drama if you two are only adding to it.'

Even though she didn't live here and had no plans to stay, Jodie gravitated towards the kettle. She needed a coffee to get over the lack of sleep, and she was sure she wouldn't be the only one in need. Jasper already had a mug of coffee in hand and was hanging around by the window nursing it.

Jodie didn't have a clue what to say to him. She'd never known anyone who'd blown hot and cold as much as he did. Only a couple of nights ago she'd confided in him over snogging a married man and he'd told her about the one-off occasion when he'd slept with Denna. Only it clearly wasn't a one-off and he wasn't acting particularly graciously just now. Surely he should be coming to Denna's aid?

'Let me,' he said, when she started lining up mugs to make everyone a drink.

'I thought you said you were never going to see her again.' Jodie realised she sounded wounded, and she was, in a way. She'd experienced too much dishonesty and tragedy since moving to London. She wanted it to end, but instead she'd been forced to listen to more lies and had ended up trapped in a box room. It turned out she preferred stints at the theatre that involved the bomb squad.

'We just bumped into each other. Same as I did with you, and I wasn't going to be rude. I didn't know she'd want to end up in bed again. Only it was the sofa because, like I said, I'm not rude. We weren't going to do it on the top bunk. Let me finish making the coffee. Everyone needs to chill out.'

In the end, there wasn't really much point in making everyone a hot drink. Once Denna had finished getting changed in the bathroom, she made her excuses and left swiftly. The two other flatmates who she didn't get to know by actual names left for work soon after. Which left Jodie nursing a coffee while Jasper had a shower, ready for his theatre shift.

The coffee had a hazelnut taste and was more comforting than usual, possibly because she'd so desperately needed it.

'Don't let last night put you off. You're free to stay again if you want to.'

Jodie had no intentions of doing that. 'I'll find somewhere else. I'll pop the key in the letterbox once I head out. I'll use the shower before I go, though, if that's okay?'

The flat, because of its limited ventilation, had a lingering smell of damp, as well as fornication. It wasn't an odour that she wanted to remain on her.

'Of course. And stay in touch this time, will ya? Last time it was as if you'd fallen off the planet.'

After he'd gone, Jodie thought about how falling off the planet seemed like a good option. The only person who might catch on to her disappearing was her sister, but she was busy doing her own thing. Other than Harper, no one else cared. She'd not met one person she could call a good friend since she'd moved here, and even though that might be entirely down to bad luck, it still meant no one would miss her.

She finished her coffee and took her shower, still musing over that fact.

She needed to come up with a plan, so she heated up one of the abandoned coffees in the microwave and took it to the single chair in the hope that hadn't been involved in the previous night's antics.

Although it was the last thing in the world she wanted to do, she needed to admit defeat. She needed to speak to her sister and let her know that all was not okay. Back when she'd been staying at the café, she'd thought she'd be able to get past it. She'd thought she'd find a part in another show and then find somewhere more secure to stay. She didn't expect to stay in another two places that only served to highlight how desperate she'd become. She didn't want to stay on another floor in another place where she wasn't certain she could trust anyone. Especially when, having stayed at places where she thought she'd been with trustworthy people, it had turned out she was entirely wrong.

Slurping half the coffee down in one go, she opened the draft message that she'd typed up to send her sister. She wondered whether she should add to it. Embellish it with details of the situation with Antoine or a rundown of what had happened because she didn't have enough cash for a place to stay.

Something told her that it was probably wise to save those details for when they saw each other. She didn't want to confess that she'd withheld things from Harper. That she'd made out her life had been better than it was, like an Instagram photo that only showed the sunny, tidy part of someone's life.

Jodie pressed send on the message. In a way, it felt like one of the bravest things she'd ever done. She'd never been able to admit to struggling before this moment.

She stared at her phone for a minute before finishing her drink. After that, she paced the small flat. She didn't want to stay here, but in the absence of an immediate reply from her sister, she didn't know what to do with herself. It seemed silly to amble around the streets when it would be hours before anyone returned to the flat.

Instead, she heated up the third and fourth cups of coffee and drank them quickly. It seemed a shame to waste them, especially when they were hitting the spot. This time when she sat down, the tiredness hit her. She was so exhausted she even risked lying down on the sofa, after a quick inspection. Her sleep patterns had been so varied in the past couple of weeks. And last night had been one of the worst.

She had her phone on so she'd be able to answer her sister when she called. A nap was exactly what she needed. And when she woke, she'd head out of the flat, hopefully with a plan in place.

It didn't take Jodie long to drift to sleep because she was unnaturally tired. Even after four cups of coffee, she didn't have the energy to combat the snoozy sensation taking over.

At the moment, sleep seemed to be the answer. Little did she know that her sleepiness wasn't because of tiredness – it was because of what Jasper had added to the coffees. And who knew whether the amount was too much to allow her ever to wake again.

CHAPTER FORTY-TWO

HARPER

Judgement day! The list of selected dancers is being put on the noticeboard at nine. I've been awake for hours and time doesn't seem to be moving.

Harper was surprised at how much value one piece of paper held and what it could mean for her future.

She'd spent the whole night thinking about it and assessing what it meant. This, for her, was a new beginning and she knew that if her name wasn't on the board, she'd be devastated. She knew there'd be other opportunities, but it was important that life didn't hold her back more than it already had.

Given that there were more modern ways to put out such information these days, it made Harper laugh that this was how they were choosing to share the news. Especially since those waiting for the news couldn't jostle to get closer to the notice-board. They were all wheelchair users who didn't want to damage their chairs or hands. So instead of a huddle, they were queuing neatly.

They were managing polite chitchat about how they'd done and what the weather was like today. The most tortuous part was trying to gauge the reactions of those further up the queue as to whether they were on the list or not.

Like she had prior to the performance, rather than concentrate on what was happening to other people, Harper started imagining how she would react when she found out. She was aiming for a poker face. If she was in, she didn't want to cheer, and if she was out, she didn't want to cry. Not here, anyway. She'd save that for later, when she was back in her own quiet room.

Planning how she would react wasn't making the queue move any faster. If she were that way inclined, she'd overtake to find out straightaway, but she figured that might get her taken out if she was in. When she'd finally made it to the front, she went from the bottom of the list to the top. With the surname Quinlan, it was always the quicker way to find out if she was listed, given that most were done alphabetically.

Harper Quinlan.

Her surname jumped out at her, its distinctiveness making it easy to find. Whatever she'd practised in her mind quickly went out of the window as she let out a small '*Yeah!*' before wheeling off to celebrate elsewhere. She didn't want to gloat in front of anyone who might not have been as successful. She also didn't want to hang around to mollycoddle anyone who hadn't made it. She'd done that previously when they'd been at university and had soon learnt that it tended to erase her own joy. Unsuccessful candidates had the tendency to bring the mood down, not cheer those who'd been successful. And after everything she'd been through to get to this point, she wanted to celebrate.

'Siri, call Maceo!'

If calling her sister was an option, Jodie would have been

first on her list. But instead it was the person who'd helped her with her rehabilitation. She hadn't known how long it would take, and her previous training had helped her immensely, but here she was after her first successful audition since becoming disabled. Maceo had helped her focus at times when she'd been close to giving up. Okay, so there had been a few distractions from him, but it hadn't stopped her, and as her phone dialled Maceo inside her pocket, she knew he was the person she wanted to celebrate with.

He picked up after three rings. 'What's the news?'

'I'm on the list.' She'd messaged him several times last night to share the agony of waiting.

'That's amazing! And do you want to hear some more good news?'

'What's that?'

'I'm in London. I was due to come down for some training so I came down to check in early. That way I could come and see you whatever the outcome was.'

'That's amazing!' She was desperate to celebrate and the fact that the person she wanted to do that with was nearby was the cherry on the cake.

'Shall I come to you? Or is there somewhere you'd like to meet?'

Harper hadn't thought about it too much. She'd not allowed her thoughts to venture towards the fact she might be celebrating. 'Can we meet at the South Bank? I've only been up there the once to meet Jodie and there are about one hundred restaurants to try. I have a craving for dumplings.'

'That sounds good to me. I'll see you there around eleven?'

That was that. Their meeting to celebrate the news was arranged. And Harper decided not to worry about whether it could be considered a date or not. She'd realised she wanted Maceo to be part of her life. And before, even though she'd claimed it was so she didn't lose focus, she'd also been scared.

She hadn't realised it but so much had altered it also involved changes in her own confidence.

Some of it had been knocked out of her during the crash, but now, slowly, one achievement at a time, she had a feeling it was going to come back.

CHAPTER FORTY-THREE

JODIE

The first time Jodie threw up, it was mostly fluid, and it seeped into the sofa. She barely knew it had happened. It was like one of those dreams in which it was impossible to place whether it was set in reality or not. Like the times she'd thought she'd heard a shout in the middle of the night, but once she was awake she had no idea whether it was real or her imagination.

No one was around to see what was happening. No one knew that Jasper had added drugs to each of the drinks – presumably so they'd all be in a much better mood for the rest of the day as he'd reasoned that caffeine alone wasn't going to fix their moods.

Jodie hadn't realised that by drinking the remaining coffees, she was inadvertently overdosing. She'd not cottoned on to the flavour, and that her mood and the resulting tiredness were not down to lack of sleep. That, in fact, it was too many narcotics entering her system at once. So her brain didn't tell her she was in danger. Not when she was too busy telling it she was just overtired. It was that. Nothing more.

The second time she vomited, it wasn't just fluid. It was her stomach contents. It was several days of reduced-price sandwiches coming up to greet her. Only she wasn't lucid enough to say hello.

Instead, it became a coagulated pool beside her mouth. One that, if anyone was about, would have been cleaned up straight-away. But there it stayed, and if she moved the wrong way, it would close her windpipe.

Because sometimes, despite trying our best, the world has a tendency to turn against us and all we can do is keep fighting. But as Jodie slipped into unconsciousness, that was no longer an option.

CHAPTER FORTY-FOUR

HARPER

The journey into London seemed quicker now she knew which way to go. Harper knew the platforms to head for and which lifts to use. She'd not had to look at her phone for clues or directions and she'd managed to arrive at the South Bank early.

She didn't mind. It gave her a while to appreciate the view and absorb the news. She *was* going to be in a show. She'd managed to speak to her dance teacher before leaving and had learnt that there were going to be three rehearsals a week for the next couple of months. As that went over her allocated time at the facility, they were going to look to increase it until after the show. Even though initially it had been quiet at the facility, she'd become used to her accommodation and actually preferred having her own space and time to herself. As a twin, it wasn't really something she'd experienced.

Thinking about Jodie left her with her an uneasy feeling. Perhaps because she should be celebrating with her twin sister. It almost felt disloyal to have told Maceo first. She realised she should have saved her three sentences until after she'd found out. Now she'd have to wait until tomorrow.

She pulled out her phone and saw that Jodie had replied to

her earlier nervous message. Expecting the usual three lines, it was a surprise to see the words *It's too Tom Hardy.*

It was the trigger sentence they'd decided on a few weeks ago when they'd met on the South Bank. Knowing that it meant Jodie wanted to talk, it was a delight to have a reason to call her. As she'd let her know about the audition, maybe she was eager to find out what had happened. It made her feel bad for not telling her already, but now was as good a time as any.

She called through while keeping an eye out for Maceo. It was a busy place, but at least she was one of the few people on the same level as him. It would make him easier to pick out from the crowd.

As she scanned around, the phone rang at the other end until it cut off to Jodie's voicemail. There weren't many times when she'd called her sister and she hadn't answered. So rather than leave a message, she tried again. When she didn't answer, she checked when the message had arrived. It was from an hour ago.

There could be any number of reasons why Jodie hadn't answered. It wasn't so long ago that she'd asked them to stick with their six-week separation. That had been the last time she'd not taken a call, but this was different. Harper was sure of it.

'Hello, showgirl! Where are we going to celebrate?' Maceo had arrived and managed to hug her before she'd even stopped staring at her phone to work out what to do. The moment the element of fear had kicked in, she'd stopped perusing the crowds for him.

'Nowhere,' she said.

'How come? I thought you wanted to have dumplings?'

Currently, her appetite had sunk as low as the basin of the River Thames. Food was very far from her mind.

'This might sound silly, but my twinstinct has been set off.'

'How come? Has something happened?'

'She texted me this.' Harper showed Maceo the text message.

'I didn't know you were both Tom Hardy fans.'

'We are, but that's not what it's about. We said we'd use that sentence if either of us wanted to speak to each other before my rehab stay was over. It was supposed to only be used in an emergency. So, now she's used it, she's not answering her phone.'

'Do you think she's in trouble?'

'I *know* she is.'

'How can you be so sure?'

Harper shrugged. She couldn't articulate why, but she was certain. 'I just know I need to get hold of her before I can sit down for a meal.'

'Let's do that, then. Do you wanna try her one more time?'

Harper tried again, feeling it would be futile but willing her sister to answer all the same. 'Nothing.'

'Do you know where she's staying? Or where she's working?'

'No. She's been auditioning. She did say she was trying for usher jobs, so we could try at the theatre where she was performing before. At least some of the people there might know where she is.'

Maceo turned to go back in the direction he'd come from.

'The Tube won't be quick enough.' She could count the number of lifts they'd have to wait for and sometimes it wasn't as simple as pressing a button. 'We need to get a taxi.'

Fortunately, as they were able to transfer out of their chairs, a London cab with a driver willing to load their chairs for them would do the trick. When they scored gold with the first cabbie they flagged, Harper breathed a little easier. But not much, because how could she, knowing her sister had sent that message but was opting not to answer her phone. Or, there was every chance that she couldn't. She didn't know why she was thinking like that, but an alarming sixth sense was telling her it was true. That she needed to be worried.

Hopefully someone at the theatre would be able to tell Harper more. Because as a twin, she'd experienced a divide. She'd become two versions of herself. And now, for the first time in their lives, they were having to live separately. And Harper's gut told her something wasn't right.

Even though this was a faster method of transportation, the traffic meant the journey was more stop–start than if they'd been on the Tube. It was frustrating as hell, but as they continued in relative silence, Harper reminded herself that there might be nothing wrong. Jodie might have just been having a slightly irrational moment, but like the last time she hadn't been able to get hold of her sister, she was full of concern.

When they arrived at the theatre, they asked the cab driver to wait. She knew the tariff would rack up, but if they found out where Jodie was staying, Harper wanted to be able to head off straightaway. The theatre itself was pretty quiet. The foyer was at the end of a long, wide corridor and when they reached it, there didn't appear to be anyone at the desk. It was one of the old-fashioned ones without accessibility in mind.

'Hello?' Maceo hollered out and it echoed in the corridor. Hopefully that would summon someone from wherever they were hidden.

'Good morning. How can I help you?' A woman's head popped up at the counter. She looked like she might have been snoozing with her head pressed against the keyboard.

'Yes, hello, I need to get hold of my sister.'

'Oh my! You must mean Jodie.'

'Yes.'

'You're her absolute double. I didn't realise she had a sister. A twin, if I'm not mistaken?'

'Yes. She wanted me to call her, only she's not answering

her phone. I'm worried something's happened. Do you know where she might be?'

'Oh, Jodie hasn't been working here for a while. She left when the pantomime did.'

'I was just hoping someone here might know how to get in touch with her...'

The woman scratched her head. 'She was working at that café at lunch times. Vincenzo's is a couple of blocks away. If not, speak to Jasper. I think she's stayed with him a few times.'

'Where's Jasper?'

'He's stocking up the kiosk. He's probably in the storeroom. I'll give him a call.' The woman spoke into a walkie-talkie, summoning Jasper to the box office, stating someone was waiting for him.

Harper turned to Maceo, who was busy on his phone. 'We've got other places to go and try and someone who might know where she is. Try not to panic,' he reassured her calmly.

Harper was doing nothing but panic. She was even sweating, which she only ever did while working out. 'What are you looking up?'

'I'm trying to find where this Vincenzo's is located. Once we've spoken to this Jasper, we can split up and look in different places.'

It made sense, but it only increased her sense of panic. A guy walked into the foyer, dragging his heels as if he was worried about what might be awaiting him.

'Jasper?' Harper said, to get his attention.

'Jodie? Shit, what's happened to you?'

Harper was certain this wouldn't be the last time there'd be confusion. If people didn't know that Jodie had an identical twin sister, they'd naturally conclude that she was Jodie. 'I'm Harper. Jodie's twin sister. I'm trying to get hold of her.'

'Twin? Shit, sorry. The pair of you look so alike I thought...

Never mind what I thought. She stayed at mine last night. She might still be there.'

Trying not to dwell on Jasper's reaction, Harper focussed on the fact that he knew where Jodie had stayed last night. 'What's the address? Can I go and check she's still there?'

'Sure. I've got a spare key. I'll go and grab it.'

'At least we know where she was last night,' Maceo said.

Harper knew she should be relieved, but she wasn't feeling it yet. There was an unexplained tension in her spine, even in the parts she could no longer feel.

'It just doesn't tell us why she's not answering her phone.'

'No, but hopefully we'll know soon and can get back to celebrating your news. I've located the café on my phone. It's only a few streets away. I'll go there and you can take the cab to wherever the flat is.'

'Good plan,' Harper said, giving a nod at the same time.

Maceo set off while she hung around for Jasper to return. He was taking far longer than she would have liked, but given the size of the theatre he might have a mile to walk to get to his locker and back. As the minutes ticked by, she was ready to explode.

She moved her chair backwards and forwards in her equivalent of pacing. The woman's head had disappeared again so Harper was alone with her despair. She decided to try phoning Jodie again. Once. Twice. Three times. Still no answer.

When the door did finally open again, Harper spun over to it. She didn't want to waste any more time.

'I've written the address on this piece of paper. She didn't get much rest last night so hopefully she's just got her phone on silent and is catching up on some sleep.'

Harper wondered if it could really be that simple. That all her concern was completely unfounded. There was only one way to know for certain. She thanked him and headed off with the address and key in hand.

The traffic played the same game all the way to the flat, which was deeper in the East End of London. There were moments when Harper wondered if they would ever arrive.

When they finally arrived, Harper paid the eye-watering taxi bill and did something that she wasn't accustomed to. She said a little prayer that everything would be okay. Because right now, she believed it was needed.

She wasn't one for anything out of the ordinary, but the hairs on the back of her neck were telling her she should be worried.

CHAPTER FORTY-FIVE

JODIE

It only takes three minutes of the brain being deprived of oxygen for it to fail. For its light to go out.

Jodie remained unaware of the predicament she was in. She was unconscious to the point that dreams didn't exist. She didn't even feel it when she was sick for a third time, leaving her airway blocked.

Life could be the pits sometimes. The cosmos working against a person, even though they were doing their best to get by.

Jodie had only dabbled in drug use. She'd managed to step away from it. And now she'd inadvertently taken more than a human was supposed to. A quadruple dose. And now one of those three precious minutes had gone.

One minute without taking a breath.

One minute of not knowing the danger she was in.

One minute closer to never breathing again.

CHAPTER FORTY-SIX

HARPER

Thus far, Harper hadn't had any major accessibility issues. The hospital and the rehabilitation centres were designed for wheelchair access. And beyond that, everywhere else she'd been had offered some accessible options, as they were used by hundreds, even thousands, of people daily. She'd not yet been to an individual domestic property catering only for the people who lived there. So arriving at a flat above a fried chicken takeaway in the heart of Leytonstone was an immediate wake-up call to some of the obstacles she might face over the years to come.

Harper reminded herself that she'd built her strength up to a level where she wasn't going to let such things get in the way, but when a passer-by offered to help her over the threshold when she'd unlocked the door, she wasn't going to be so stubborn that she wouldn't accept the help.

'Hello...? Jodie, are you here?'

She'd made it inside, but she'd not made it to her sister. If she was here at all. There was a stairwell in the way of her finding out. No lifts. No ramps. Just thirteen steps up to the flat.

'Jodie, are you there?'

No answer. The stairs seemed like a lot to combat if she was in the wrong place.

Harper decided to try the thing she'd been attempting all along and rang her sister again. Upstairs, the ringing sounded out.

'Jodie?' Harper couldn't work out if she'd just left her mobile here, or if something far worse had happened.

Realising that as far as her sister was concerned, her instincts were rarely wrong, she abandoned her chair and began to make her way up the stairs on her backside. It went against some of the advice she'd been given, but the situation and the concern she was holding called for drastic action. As she reached the third step, she heard a gentle moan.

'Jodie, is that you?'

There was no further sound. Harper kept going, but it seemed to be taking forever. For each step she placed her bottom on, she had to check it with her hands first to ensure there was nothing that might damage her skin.

Because her nervous system was no longer wired up like it should be, she had to protect her skin more than the average person. If she got a nick or a scrape, especially without realising, it could cause her more problems. Whereas an intact nervous system would recoil at sitting on a pin, hers wouldn't even know that it had. Even the carpet grippers that were sometimes used on stairs would be enough to cause untold damage if she were to sit on them directly.

As quickly as possible, she investigated each step before bumping herself carefully onto the next one. The only thing she couldn't control was how her lower legs landed. She tried not to let the whole process slow her down.

It was only once she was halfway up that she cottoned on to the fact she'd left her wheelchair behind. It should have been fairly evident from the start given that these days it was like an appendage, but in her rush, she'd not thought about what she would do once she got to the top. It was too late to worry; getting to the top was the main thing. With each step that she checked, she shouted Jodie's name. It felt important even though it might turn out she was whistling in the wind with no one there to hear.

A cough. A splutter.

This time the sound was definite. Not imagined or dreamt up. It was the sound of someone in trouble. And not just anyone, it was her twin sister. The other half of her. Giving up the rigmarole of sensible precautions, she instead took the risk of a cut or scrape. That didn't seem to matter anymore. She might take longer to heal, but she would heal. Only she wouldn't if anything happened to Jodie.

She reached the landing, but without her chair she had to continue bridging herself along, bringing her lower limbs with her. Thankfully, there was only one direction available, a single door to go through. She pushed it open and backed her way into the room. Turning to look, she was presented with something she never wanted to see.

Jodie must have felt the same thing when she'd witnessed Harper's accident. That moment when the world falls apart. Only, when it had been Harper in trouble there'd been an untold number of people on hand to deal with the emergency. And here, Harper was on her own. The only person able to help her sister.

'Siri, call 999.' If there was one thing she had perfected, it was the ability to make hands-free phone calls. Her hands were usually occupied while she was wheeling, so she'd taken to storing her phone in her top pocket so voice activation was always picked up. Fortunately, it started to ring as she made her way over.

'Jodie, it's Harper. I'm here. Don't worry. I'm here for you.' When she reached the sofa, her sister was on her back, a pool of vomit by her side. 'Oh, Jodie, what's happened?'

But, of course, her sister didn't answer.

Using all her strength, Harper drew her into the recovery position. Jodie coughed and spluttered.

'That's it, sweetie, get it out of your system.'

'Hello. What's your emergency?' an efficient voice said from the other end of the phone.

'Ambulance. I need an ambulance. My sister's unconscious and she's been throwing up.'

It didn't take long for the woman to get the details she needed. It included instructions for Harper to check her sister's breathing and pulse.

She was breathing. Just.

That meant Harper didn't have to work out how to perform resuscitation when kneeling wasn't an option. She'd do whatever was required, though, to make sure her sister was okay.

Harper stroked Jodie's back, murmuring words of comfort as she did.

'Help will be here soon. The ambulance is on its way.'

Jodie wasn't responsive enough for Harper to ask what had caused her to become unwell, and there weren't any obvious clues about. No alcohol bottles or pill pots. It might be something as simple as food poisoning. Harper had no way of knowing, so she couldn't answer some of the phone operator's questions.

She felt bad about that. This was her sister. And not only her sister, her *twin*. A duplicate of her DNA. Normally she knew everything about her life. As far as she was aware from the messages she'd been receiving, Jodie was auditioning for a new job and had started dating her beau from the café. That information was obviously lacking based on the scene in front of her now.

The sound of sirens was music to her ears and she hoped Jodie was able to hear them as well, to know that help was here and she was going to be taken care of. Harper had experienced that relief when her face had been pressed against a pavement with everyone insisting she didn't move. She put that to the back of her mind. Reliving her own trauma wasn't going to help right now. She needed to concentrate on reassuring her sister and willing her to be okay.

Two paramedics made it to the top of the stairs with heavy kitbags on their shoulders. They asked similar questions to those of the woman on the telephone, some of which Harper was again unable to answer.

'And the wheelchair is yours?' one of them asked to clarify.

'Yep. T12 complete paraplegic. We're identical apart from that.'

'And you don't know what's caused this?'

'No. I've been at rehab so we haven't seen each other for a few weeks. She wanted me to call her and when she didn't answer it made me worry so I came here.'

Harper didn't like to think about what might have happened if she hadn't. The other paramedic was busy clearing Jodie's airway and placing a plastic tube in her mouth.

'It's to ensure her airway remains clear,' he said when he caught Harper observing his every move. 'Everything's stable, but we need to work out why she's not as awake as we'd like her to be.'

'I'll go and get the stretcher,' the second paramedic said as more medics arrived to help.

With all the toing and froing, Harper moved herself out of the way, thankful that she had the strength to lever herself into a chair.

'We're going to set off shortly. Are you going to be okay? Do you have anyone you can call?'

Foolishly, Harper hadn't checked her phone. It had been on silent all day, hence why she hadn't seen her sister's message straightaway, but thankfully she had been able to respond in the nick of time.

'I'll call my friend. Where should we head?'

'We're going to Whipps Cross. Do you need any assistance?'

'No. You concentrate on my sister. Make her better for me.'

Watching Jodie being taken away was one of the worst things she'd witnessed in her life, although finding her here in the first place would trump that. She just had to hope the day wouldn't get any worse.

CHAPTER FORTY-SEVEN

JODIE

In the second minute Jodie managed a cough. In the third, there was something calling her. An angel shouting her name. Soothing her soul. After that she was being pulled and poked. Lights were being waggled in her eyes, and items were prodding her mouth, and before she knew it she was floating.

She'd always wanted the ability to fly. To be able to soar above places to see what was going on. To watch concerts from the best seat in the house. But this wasn't the kind that she'd dreamt of. It was the kind that made her nauseous, as if she were on a bad boat trip. One where everyone got seasick. Except that she was the only one on the boat. There was no one else about. Only her.

The idea that she might be completely alone in the world filled her with despair. She'd never been fully alone. Even in the womb she'd had company. And although they'd not been as close in recent weeks, they'd still been in touch, still exchanged daily messages.

Soon, she was no longer flying but racing. Jodie sensed the motion, but for the life of her she couldn't open her eyelids. They were as reluctant as a teenager was to get out of bed in the morning. No matter how she tried to persuade them, she couldn't get them to move.

That sensation was soon overtaken by an alien abduction. The prodding and poking started up again. She tried to yell for it all to stop, but someone had put a pebble in her mouth, making it hard to form words. Instead, she was making slurring sounds that not even she could understand.

She tried to bat the aliens off. She didn't want to be kidnapped. She wanted to open her eyes and see her sister and for everything to be back to how it was. Only not the version that included some of the people she'd thought of as friends.

And then the wooziness started. Even woozier than before. Holding her in a place where the only important thing was sleep. Rest. The chance to recover.

CHAPTER FORTY-EIGHT

HARPER

Harper had stayed by Jodie's bedside ever since she'd arrived with Maceo. He was in the visitors' waiting room. Harper didn't want him to meet her sister before she was conscious again. She wanted to afford her sister that dignity.

The doctors had sedated Jodie to allow what was in her system to be expelled with their help, and then they were going to wake her up gradually to assess whether there had been any permanent damage. There had been talk of a scan, but all Harper could focus on was her sister's face. The one that was hers as well. The long blonde hair that they'd always kept the same length. The crystal-blue eyes that would occasionally flicker open. Her face would have looked angelic if it weren't for the tube poking from her mouth.

What Harper didn't understand was why Jodie hadn't told her. If she'd been using drugs then why hadn't she said? They'd always shared everything. Until recently. Harper blamed herself. She blamed herself because she'd not wanted to be able to draw a comparison between the two of them. Not for a while at least. It hadn't been so long ago that Harper had been the one having a medical crisis. She'd been the one who had required emergency surgery to stabilise her back. But everything had ended up destabilised ever since, for her and her sister. They'd not been in each other's pockets like they had before. They'd not spent practically every minute of every day in each other's company. It upset Harper on a level that was hard to explain.

So Harper held her sister's hand and hoped that Jodie knew she was there. That she planned to never not be there again.

They were Harper and Jodie. Jodie and Harper. She didn't know what she'd do if the other half of her didn't wake up.

CHAPTER FORTY-NINE

JODIE

Waking up wasn't a one-day affair for Jodie. It was like she was a butterfly emerging from a chrysalis. Certain things had needed to occur before the next one could happen. Not unlike Harper's experience, it was apparently a few days before they'd known she was breathing without help and compos mentis enough to know what was going on. Harper had been there every minute since Jodie had started to wake up. And ever since she'd opened her eyes and recognised her sister, she'd known there was a question waiting.

'Why didn't you tell me, sweetie?' Harper asked when she was sitting up after having her swallow assessed and her first proper food.

'What do you mean?' Jodie's disorientation over the past few days extended to not knowing what her sister was on about. 'Tell you what?'

'About what you've been getting into. Antoine told Maceo that you'd been using... *drugs*.' Harper said the last word in a whisper, as if she didn't want anyone else to hear.

'What? That was only a few times and when I realised I was becoming dependent on them, Antoine helped me give up.'

'He said that you'd gone back to it and it was bound to be the cause. When the doctors checked, you had drugs in your system.'

'That cheating scumbag can go and live under a rock!' Jodie croaked. 'When I get out of here, I'm going to go and shout at him like I should have done when I found out he has a wife.'

'Pardon?'

'Yes, after taking me for a romantic trip to Brighton and kissing me, it was our boss that let me know that Antoine in fact has a wife. Not that it matters now. What did you say about drugs in my system?' Considering she'd been out of it for a while, it was surprising how easily fury arrived. She hadn't spoken to Antoine since she'd left the café – how dare he presume to know anything about her life.

'The doctors checked, given what Antoine told us, and they found a large amount of amphetamine in your system. They assumed it was an overdose, but they had no way of knowing whether it was intentional or not.'

'I didn't take any drugs. Not this time.' Jodie had been at a low point, but she'd refused to go there again.

'You should have told me. I would have helped you.'

Jodie was too busy shaking her head, her comprehension trying to catch up. Had she taken it and not remembered? No, she wouldn't have. She was sure of it.

'Coffee!' she suddenly blurted out loud.

'I can go and get you one if you want?' Harper offered.

'No, no, not that. I'm not sure I'll ever want to drink coffee again. That morning, Jasper made coffee for everyone. When I drank mine I thought it had an unusual taste, but I liked it so I drank three more. It must have been laced with something and if they all had it, then it's no wonder I was ill. I know I got myself in a bit of a rut, but I'd got over that.'

Jodie knew it was true as soon as she said it. No doubt Jasper hadn't said a thing to save his own arse. The coffee mugs would have been cleaned and other evidence removed so there was no danger of a finger being pointed in his direction. One thing she'd learnt over the past few months was not to trust everyone. That some people only had their own interests at heart.

'I thought it sounded off. And I like to think that I know you better than anyone else. I don't intend for anyone or anything to get between us ever again.'

'Not even Maceo?'

'Especially not Maceo, but he knows that I don't let anything get in my way.' Harper's cheeks flushed slightly. 'It doesn't mean that I don't like him, though.'

'Does that mean I'm going to be allowed to meet him, then? You can't leave him waiting outside forever.'

'You don't mind?'

'I don't mind, if you don't. And do me a favour... before he comes in, let him know that everything Antoine told him wasn't true. I don't think that man knows how to be honest.'

It made Jodie sad to think that without her sister around, her judgement had been chronically poor. The friends she'd made through the show hadn't been a good influence and had nearly ended up killing her. Her friendship with a work colleague that she'd thought was going to turn into a romance resulted in her finding out he was married, and somehow she'd been the one to lose her job.

Still, like her sister previously, she was still upright. She was still alive. She planned not to waste a moment. She wasn't sure how it would work, but she also never wanted to be without her sister again. Some people were meant to be together and they certainly were. It was a promise they'd made to each other and managed to keep. Just.

'Oh my, at long last! What an honour it is to meet my future sister-in-law! I am Maceo. So nice to meet you!' Maceo wheeled over to her so quickly that Jodie struggled to keep up with everything he was saying.

Harper was in his wake and glaring in his direction.

'I didn't... have you...?' Jodie glanced from one to the other, wondering how she'd missed news of a proposal.

'No, Jodie. Don't worry, you would have been the first to know. Maceo just likes to get massively ahead of himself.' Harper placed a hand on his knee as if to steady his announcements.

The gesture made Jodie smile because she'd never much believed in holding back. 'I'm Jodie and I'm absolutely delighted to meet my future brother-in-law.'

Harper shook her head again, but smiled as she did. 'Why are you two so impossible?'

'Ah, but you wouldn't be without us, would you?'

And in the same way that she knew a brother-in-law was on the cards, she also knew they wouldn't be without each other. Because neither of them would ever want that again.

Jodie and Harper.

Harper and Jodie.

All was right with the world.

EPILOGUE

As humans, there are times when we need to be together. And there are times when we need to be apart. Sometimes we love spending time with those under our roofs, but there are times when having a house to ourselves is the biggest luxury.

Being apart had been a temporary necessity for Jodie and Harper. And in that time, they'd changed the way they looked at dreams. Because sometimes life needed to be re-evaluated. They'd thought their dream of being on stage together was over, but it turned out to be just the beginning.

As Jodie recovered, Harper rehearsed ready for her first time on stage since starting to use a wheelchair. For the final performance, Jodie, her parents and Maceo were in the audience cheering her on.

Then Jodie and Harper returned to auditioning together. The way they'd always intended.

It took less than two weeks for them to be offered two chorus places. And this time, it wasn't on the peripheries in some unknown show. This time it was in the West End. Because they'd learnt to dance together. They came as a pair. It was the most unique thing the director had seen, and the offer came on the spot.

And even though some things hadn't worked out like they'd expected, they didn't look back until Harper was one of the first wheelchair users to take the lead in a West End show. It took years, but they got there, their parents ensuring they attended the first and last performance of every show, with some international travel for them in between.

'Are we going to join the end-of-show drinks?' Jodie asked at the end of their last performance in London before the show toured the country, with them in tow. This time, it was their turn to travel.

'I'm not sure.'

It wasn't the first time Harper had hesitated about joining the occasion. After all, the first time they'd done so, or attempted to, it hadn't worked out like anyone would have wanted.

'I think we should. After all, once we set off we're not going to be in London for quite some time.' The tour they were joining was a year-long programme, the show proving so popular that other theatres were calling out to host it.

'You're right. I need to get over that.'

'Definitely. Everyone's waiting. I'll see you in the foyer once you're ready.'

Harper got herself out of her costume and took a moment to reflect and appreciate how far they'd both come. Sometimes it was easy to forget how far that was.

When she finally reached the foyer, the cast were standing oddly. Well, it wouldn't have been odd if they were on the stage. This was the formation they took for the final piece and as soon as she'd registered that fact, they started dancing as if they were on stage and the music was still playing.

Maceo was in Harper's place, and it took a few manoeuvres for it to dawn on her exactly what was going on.

'Not again!' she said.

'Oh, you know I'm going to do it as many times as it takes. So, are you ready?'

'Ready?' This was Maceo's third marriage proposal. She hadn't said no on either of the two previous occasions. She'd just said she wasn't ready and it was too soon.

'Yes. I know not to ask unless you are ready.'

'Will you marry me?' she said.

'Pardon?'

'You heard me! I must be ready if it's me asking you.'

Everyone burst into more dance while Maceo and Harper kissed, and even though it kind of spoilt the moment, Jodie wrapped her arms around them both. Until she found her plus one, she was quite happy to be their gooseberry. Because if life had taught her anything, it was to keep the people she loved and trusted close.

And if life had taught Harper anything, it was to trust her instincts.

Or in this case, her twinstincts.

A LETTER FROM CATHERINE

Dear Reader,

As the daughter of a disabled mother and someone with a chronic illness, I realised I needed to write a story that recognised that disability should become the hero. It's not always portrayed in that light, and knowing many disabled heroes in my own life meant I wanted to create a fictional one. I have always tried to include disability and chronic illness in my books and will continue to do so. I also wanted to highlight that we don't always know what's happening in another person's life. What we're being told might not be the whole story, and it's important to be there for each other, especially with everything that has occurred over the past few years.

If you did enjoy *A Life Lived Beautifully* and want to keep up to date with all my latest releases, just sign up at the following link. Your email address will never be shared and you can unsubscribe at any time.

www.bookouture.com/catherine-miller

I hope you loved *A Life Lived Beautifully* and if you did, I would be very grateful if you could write a review. Every one of them is appreciated. I'd love to hear what you think, and it makes such a difference in helping new readers discover my books for the first time.

I love hearing from my readers – you can get in touch on my Facebook page, through Twitter, Goodreads or my website.

If you have a sibling, go and give them a call. If not, I hope you're lucky enough to find friends who are as good as.

Love, happiness and thanks,

Catherine x

www.katylittlelady.com

facebook.com/katylittlelady.author

twitter.com/katylittlelady

instagram.com/katylittlelady

ACKNOWLEDGEMENTS

I'm writing this only three weeks after marrying Ben! My long-time partner who has been there for my twin girls and me through thick and thin. We were really blessed with the day we celebrated and I'd like to extend thanks to all of Ben's family for welcoming us with open arms, and to all the people who helped make the day go so smoothly. Also, to Ben for putting up with me. It's a mutual thing and the reason we're in love!

When I originally came up with the idea for this story, I imagined it as one life told two different ways. A story about a life with and without disability and how one shouldn't be better than the other. It ended up being told as a story of twin sisters and I'm really pleased with how it's turned out. I hope you've enjoyed it as well. You can see some of my experience as a former physiotherapist coming through. My time working for the NHS and the care I have received since have helped mould this novel.

I'd like to thank my agent, Hattie Grunewald, and my editors, Jess Whitlum-Cooper and Christina Demosthenous, who've all helped shape this story. Alongside them, I'd also like to thank my copy editor, Angela Snowden; proofreader, Becca Allen; Mandy Kullar, in managing editorial; and the rest of the Bookouture team.

During the process of writing this book, I applied to be a co-editor for the next Disabled Issue of *The Bookseller*. As I stated in my letter in this book, I've lived a life surrounded by and working with disability and chronic illness, and so it's something I've been passionate about long-term. Thank you to Book-outure for supporting me in doing this, and thank you to my fellow co-editors, Claire Wade and Nydia Hetherington, for being great colleagues during the process of getting the Disabled Issue ready.

Last, I'd like to thank you. For reading this novel and getting this far. Books are just words until they are read, and I'm so thankful for all my readers. A special thanks to those who've read one of my books and decided to read more. It's one of the best feelings as a writer to know that readers have enjoyed a story enough to want to read more and I can't quite believe the publication of this book means I've reached double figures! If you've loved my tenth book, do check out the rest and tell your friends. I'll be forever thankful!

Ingram Content Group UK Ltd.
Milton Keynes UK
UKHW010049100623
423157UK00003B/20

9 781837 909087